Darcy Does Dallas

A Gay *Pride and Prejudice* Variation

Andrea Dalling

I0624346

Darcy Does Dallas by Andrea Dalling.
© 2019 Andrea Dalling.
Paperback Edition,
ISBN 978-1-942198-18-5.
Edited by Lori Parks.
Cover design by Artesian Well Publishing.

All rights reserved. No part of this story may be used, reproduced or transmitted in any form or by any means without written permission of the copyright holder, except in the case of brief quotations embodied within critical reviews and articles.

This book is a work of fiction. The names, characters, places, and incidents are products of the writer's imagination or have been used fictitiously and are not to be construed as real. Any resemblance to persons, living or dead, actual events, locale or organizations is entirely coincidental.

The author has asserted her rights under the Copyright Designs and Patents Acts 1988 (as amended) to be identified as the author of this book.

This book contains sexually explicit content which is suitable only for mature readers.

First electronic publication: November 2019.
LoveLight Press

Darcy Does Dallas is set in the U.S. and uses American English.

Table of Contents

About This Book

Ten years ago, his first love betrayed him. Is a spark still left among the ashes?

CEO Will Darcy has spent the past decade putting thoughts of George Wickham out of his mind. His childhood friend grew up to be a compulsive drinker and gambler, wasting every opportunity Will's father had given him. Seeing him again on a business trip to Dallas brings up old memories of the heat between them, but Will is over that heartbreak. He's got a corporate merger to wrap up. There's no time to wallow in thoughts of what might have been.

George Wickham has no idea of the secret merger planned between his company and Pemberley Industries—not until a colleague's emergency brings Geo onto the transition team. Without warning, he's in face-to-face negotiations with the only man he ever loved. The man he let down so completely, forgiveness is impossible. Behind the anger in Will's soulful dark eyes, could a hint of desire still burn?

When they're forced to work together for the good of their companies, the emotions that bubble up in the boardroom soon overflow into the bedroom. Is this just a fling to sate their carnal impulses? Or can they learn to trust again?

This scorching M/M romance novella is for a mature audience. It has a happy ending and no cliffhanger.

Chapter 1

I t's a universal truth that if a business trip can go wrong, it will.

Weather delay, check. Lost luggage, check. No car to meet them at the airport, check.

"You can ride in an Uber like a normal person, Will." This impertinence came from the mouth of Pemberley Industries' chief counsel, Mandie Price. And a pretty mouth it was—or so Will would have thought, if he were straight.

Mandie had the look of an underwear model—tall, blonde, willowy, with hair down to her waist. She was possibly the smartest person Will had ever met. That combination made her a formidable adversary in negotiations. Beauty like hers short-circuited the brains of most men.

But Will Darcy was not most men, and he was not accustomed to his employees smart-mouthing him. He put up with it from her because she was worth it.

A gray sedan pulled up to the curb in front of baggage claim. The driver loaded their carry-ons and Mandie's checked bag into the trunk. Will's checked bag was not lost, the woman at the customer service desk had insisted. The airline just didn't know where it was.

He had tried arguing the finer points of semantics, but Mandie had rolled her eyes at him and squeezed his arm. He understood the futility of the enterprise, so he gave in. He was still rehearsing in his head all the things he wished he'd said.

Mandie looked across the car seat at him with her incisive blue gaze. "If you keep your jaw clenched like that, it will give you a headache."

"I already have a headache."

She smirked at him. "Then I guess there's no point in listening to me." She rooted through her bag, pulling out some Tylenol and an unopened bottle of water. "Take this."

He obeyed, because it was easier than arguing with her. He supposed this must be what marriage was like.

Not that Will was likely to find out anytime soon. His last relationship had ended in disaster, again. He came home early from a business trip to find his boyfriend Trevor asleep, and a strange man coming out of the shower.

Life as a CEO wasn't conducive to monogamy. He was on the road more days than he was home. His boyfriends felt neglected. Inevitably, they strayed.

Will wasn't even surprised by it anymore.

"I hate traveling," he said, a simple truth muttered under his breath, not really meant for anyone else to hear. But Mandie reached over and squeezed his hand.

It wasn't a very businesslike gesture. Mandie had been the one he called after he ordered Trevor out of his penthouse. She had taken him out and gotten him drunk. She was, he supposed, his best friend.

They drove across twenty miles of flat land to downtown Dallas. He forced himself to focus his mind on the reason for this trip. The merger would be a turning point for his company. It would make Pemberley a major player in emerging technologies that would help reverse climate change.

It was the future. And Pemberley would lead the way.

He felt good about the plans the transition team had made. They had set themselves up for success. And yet, his stomach began to churn when they reached the city.

It had nothing to do with business.

He hadn't been to this part of Texas since he was eighteen. Hadn't expected the place to bring back memories. But somehow, it did.

Memories of George Wickham, his first love. How perfect it had been. And how it had all gone to hell.

Heading toward the sights of downtown, Will's chest tightened. Images floated in his mind. The funeral. Holding Geo's hand. That night in the hotel room.

The night his world had changed.

The car lurched to a halt in front of the hotel. In a rush, Will and Mandie left their bags at the valet stand. Will handed a thick tip to the gray-haired Latino gentleman who would take their bags to their rooms at check-in time.

They were late for the meeting, and Will hated to be late. Even when his travel plans had been shot to hell, and it wasn't his fault.

Fortunately, the offices of Crisanto Software were on the next block, so they didn't have to wait for a cab. After a short walk, he and Mandie entered the professional building. They stopped to freshen up in the restrooms off the lobby.

Will let out a sigh of relief. This buyout would be good for Pemberley Industries. They'd been using Crisanto's software to operate their factory equipment for years. The smaller company's products would be a good fit with their portfolio.

The meeting that morning was a formality. The deal had been struck, and all that was left to do was sign the papers. Then would come the trickier task of merging the operations.

Will liked to involve himself personally in those decisions, at least at a high level. He hated laying off good people because of redundancies. He preferred to assimilate them into the organization in some other capacity when he could.

He brushed his fingers through his hair and adjusted his tie. His perfectly tailored suit looked neat despite the first-class plane ride. He stepped out, and Mandie soon joined him. They made their way to the elevators.

The receptionist at Crisanto placed a call, and they were immediately met by Chanisse Littleton, the CFO. A Black woman of about fifty, she was on the plump side, her dark hair highlighted with silver.

Will had gotten to know her on the conference calls over the past few months. He appreciated her quiet wisdom, the way she steered the conversation back on topic when they went off on tangents. The Crisanto CEO and his assistant were both idea people, and they often moved from point A to point 29 while everyone else was still on point B.

"How was your flight?" Chanisse asked.

"Aside from being late, it was fine, thank you."

Mandie let out a sigh. She said to Chanisse, "He's a little cranky today. If we can get him caffeinated, he should be fine."

"I don't need a nursemaid, Melinda."

"It's Amanda," she countered, "as you know, Fitzwilliam."

Chanisse chuckled. She led them into a conference room where three others waited.

A woman in her twenties with sleek black hair sat at the long wooden table. Will's eyes were immediately drawn to her fuchsia suit. She stopped keying at her computer and stood as they entered. He recognized her as Suki, the executive assistant. He shook the hand she offered.

His gaze then traveled to the dark-suited men in front of the window. His heart lost its rhythm. That man, the younger one—no, it couldn't be. It was the strangeness of being back in Dallas again. It had been ten years, after all. Would Will even recognize George Wickham if he saw him again?

The man turned toward him, and those eyes. Will could never forget those turquoise eyes. People didn't believe Geo when he said they weren't colored contact lenses. But Will knew. Will knew because they'd been friends since infancy, and Geo's eyes had always been that color, as bright and clear as the Caribbean Sea.

And that same lock of hair fell over his forehead, the one that stubbornly refused to stay in place. No matter how his mother had fussed over it when posing him for photos, that one brown curl would not be tamed.

Will expected a sudden rush of fury to rise inside him. But ten years had softened the edges of his anger. He was shocked, he was discombobulated, he was empty, but the rage refused to come.

And he needed the rage. Because right now, his body was vibrating with the memories of the other man's touch. His heart was pounding like a timpani. And his brain was screaming *mine.*

What the hell? George Wickham hadn't been his since college. They had made a clean break. After that awful night in Vegas, they'd never seen each other again.

Until now. What the fuck was Geo doing here? Will had teleconferenced with all the members of the transition team, and Geo hadn't been one of them. This merger was supposed to be kept secret until the formal announcement was made. And Geo was the least trustworthy person Will knew.

"Oscar, good to finally meet you face to face," Mandie said, addressing the Crisanto CEO. He was in his forties, of medium height, his dark hair graying at the temples. A broad smile brightened his round face.

"You as well," Oscar said. "This is George Wickham from our legal team."

She stretched out her hand. "I'm Amanda Price. You can call me Mandie. This is Will Darcy. You can call him Mr. Darcy. Everyone does."

Will shot her a look, but in truth he was grateful she had made the introductions. His brain had left the building. But he was back now. He had to be. He couldn't afford to screw up this deal.

"Good to see you," he said, shaking Oscar's hand. He looked straight into Geo's face but said nothing.

"It's an honor, Mr. Darcy," Geo said with a smirk. "Or shall I call you *your highness*?"

The sound of that voice woke something long-buried in Will—something buried so deep, he'd thought it dead. But now it resurrected, as full of life as it had ever been. And it was screaming with a desire Will couldn't escape.

He bit his cheek hard. He hadn't risen to the position of CEO of Pemberley Industries at the age of twenty-seven by letting his emotions get the best of him. True, he and his sister owned a majority of the company stock, but the board of directors had voted him in unanimously. That was five years ago, and the company was thriving under his leadership.

He would not let Geo rattle him.

"Usually, I prefer *my lord and master*," Will said. Geo flushed and looked like he might swallow his tongue. "But since we're all friends here, you can call me Will."

"Thank you. You can call me Geo," he said as he turned his gaze to Mandie.

"Where's Becca?" Will asked, referring to the Crisanto lawyer who had negotiated the deal.

"Her mother had a bad fall," Geo explained, "so Becca had to fly to Florida. She and I have been conferencing all morning to catch me up."

"Oh, I'm sorry to hear about her mom," Mandie said. "I hope she'll be okay."

"Nothing too serious," Oscar replied. "She'll need help getting around for a few days."

"In the meantime," Geo said, his tone casual, his eyes wary, "you're stuck with me. The papers are all in order, from what I understand."

"Good. Shall we get started?" Will asked. Oscar motioned for him and Mandie to take a seat.

Mandie looked through the contracts, huddling with Geo. Will chatted with Oscar while Chanisse showed Suki photos of her grandbaby. More coffee was brought in, along with an assortment of breakfast pastries.

Every few minutes, Will's eyes wandered to Geo and Mandie. He was sitting close to her, a flirtatious smile on his lips. Of course he was. Geo was bi, and no one was off limits.

Not even Will's sister.

But that was in the past. Ana was married now, finishing up her residency in pediatrics. Geo was no threat to her.

And Mandie was practically engaged. At least, that's how she had been describing herself for the past year. Will didn't know why her boyfriend hadn't put a ring on her finger yet...

She wouldn't stray, certainly. A woman like Mandie wouldn't let a smooth talker like Geo take her in. She was too smart for that.

So what was that hot, tight sensation in the pit of Will's stomach? Not jealousy, certainly. And what was taking them so long? Mandie and Becca had ironed out the contract already. The signing was supposed to be a formality.

Maybe Geo was trying to sabotage the deal. If it went through, Will would technically be his boss. Was Geo worried Will would fire him?

Would Will fire him?

The idea had its appeal. But to swoop in and shatter Geo's life ten years later over an old vendetta seemed petty. That wasn't Will's style.

Clearly Geo had worked hard and cleaned up his act. Will didn't begrudge him that. But he didn't trust him. And he didn't like the idea that Geo had any say over the future of Pemberley.

Will walked over and sat next to Mandie. "Everything all right here?"

"Geo found a couple of points where the language could be clarified."

"We'll have Suki make the changes," Geo said, "and print off new copies. Shouldn't take more than fifteen minutes."

"I want to approve the changes first," Will said.

Mandie scowled. "Of course. It's just boring legalese, though."

"Afraid I might try something nefarious?" Geo asked, oozing charm and wearing a mocking smile.

Will ought to tell Mandie the truth. About the terrible breakup, about Geo's betrayal, about the death of the friendship that had once meant everything to Will. For the first twenty-two years of their lives, they had never spent more than two weeks apart. But after that day in Vegas, they had gone ten years without seeing each other, without communicating in any way.

Ten years.

Suddenly, the weight of it felt like penance. Like a punishment for being young and stupid. For making life-altering decisions without knowing they *were* life-altering.

Will put that thought away to contemplate at a later time. He looked unabashedly into Geo's crystalline blue eyes. "*Would* you try something nefarious?"

Geo chuckled, the sound as smooth as aged whiskey. "I might. But I didn't."

"It's nothing, Will, really," Mandie stressed.

He nodded, then rose and walked to the window. The panoramic view showed the city decked out for the holidays. At night it would be even more spectacular, lights glittering against the dark sky.

When the fresh contracts were ready, Will took his seat. Mandie set the copies down in front of him and Oscar. With the flourish of a pen, Will brought Crisanto Software into the Pemberley family.

It hadn't been necessary for him to fly to Dallas for this. The documents could have been signed electronically. But the face-to-face meetings had both real and symbolic meaning for the employees of

Crisanto. Will wanted them to know he was personally invested in this merger.

"Thank you, ladies and gentlemen," Will said. "This is the culmination of many months of hard work. It's been a pleasure working with all of you. Pity Becca couldn't be here."

"Pity indeed," Geo said smoothly. Everyone laughed except Will.

Chapter 2

*O*f all the conference rooms in all the world, he had to walk into mine.

Geo stared into the man's hard expression. Will Darcy. The love of his life. His greatest regret.

And now, his boss.

Unless Will decided to eliminate Geo's position. If he did, Geo couldn't really blame him.

But Geo was finding it hard to care about that. Because he and Will were in the same room, and maybe that meant a chance for closure. A chance to show that the worst mistake of his life didn't define him.

If only the testosterone weren't fogging his brain. Because damn, Will looked good.

Ten years ought to have made a difference, but it didn't as far as Geo's libido was concerned. His body seemed to think the CEO with the broad shoulders and the brooding dark eyes was still the same boy he'd always known. The one who'd made a man of him in every way that mattered.

But this was business. Geo wouldn't jeopardize his job by doing something stupid. He would prove to Will that he was a professional. Reliable. An asset to the company.

That was a change from his younger days, when Will had known him. Back then, Geo had gotten by on charm and good looks. He'd been born knowing how to flatter and please.

That talent came in handy as the group chatted amiably. He bantered with barely a thought. Most of his brain—and his body, too—was preoccupied with Will.

At twenty-two, Will had been tall and strikingly handsome. Ten years later, as CEO of Pemberley, he was confident and imposing besides. He didn't have to take shit from anyone. And he wasn't going to take shit from Geo.

That was okay. Geo wanted a sincere conversation. Which was stupid, because what difference could it make? Geo had betrayed Will's love and trust. He had no excuse. Nothing could mitigate his actions.

The last time he had seen Will, it had been the lowest point in his life. But Geo had put that awful weekend behind him. He had moved on.

Or so he had thought. One look at Will, and Geo had found himself staring face-to-face with the shadow of his old self, that dumb kid who expected the world to hand him a living. Who envied Will's money. Who never gave a thought to the huge responsibility Will had inherited—until it was far too late to make amends.

Will had walked away from him in Vegas, one arm around his sister Ana, and hadn't given Geo a backward glance.

They hadn't seen each other since.

Not until that morning, when Will walked through that conference room door looking as gorgeous as ever. When their eyes met, Geo saw surprise there. Will had no clue Geo would be at the meeting.

That was awkward.

Oscar should have sent Will an email at least. Apparently the change in the legal rep hadn't seemed an urgent matter. But then, why would it? The papers had already been drawn up.

He wanted to bang his head on the table. What an awful coincidence this was.

The pop of a champagne cork woke Geo from his reverie. Oscar filled the glasses, but of course Geo declined. Will scowled, and Geo could read his thoughts. He was glad Geo was abstaining, but wondering if it was just for show.

They had some time before their lunch reservations. The group took a break. Everyone left the conference room except Will and Geo.

Will opened up his computer, and Geo grinned at his stoicism. The man wouldn't let Geo's presence affect him. He had too much pride for that.

Even after all these years, Geo knew him so well.

Now that they were alone, Geo had to say *something*. He was the one who had screwed up. He was the one who would have to make amends.

"I'm sorry about this." Geo was careful to keep the emotion out of his voice.

Will didn't look up. "No need to speak of it."

Geo chuckled, then said in a gently mocking tone, "Of course not. Let's pretend we never met until this morning."

Will glanced at him, a cascade of emotions playing in his eyes before he schooled his expression. He said flatly, "Have you a better suggestion?"

Geo bit his cheek. "I should start by apologizing for what happened the last time we saw each other."

"Water under the bridge."

Geo was silent a long time, working to quell the heartache of Will's dismissal. "Is that what I am to you? Water under the bridge?"

Will eyed him stonily. "What do you want me to say?"

Geo rose and walked toward him. Will's gaze followed him, dark eyes intense. Geo sat two chairs down. "I don't expect you to forgive me."

"Good."

"But we'll be working together the next two weeks." Geo stopped a moment and said in a tight voice, "Unless you want me off the project."

Will seemed to contemplate that a moment. "No need for that. We're adults."

Geo shook his head. Frustration built in his chest. "You haven't changed a bit."

"You don't know anything about me," Will said. The bitterness in his voice revealed the deep emotion he'd been trying so hard to hide.

"You can pretend we're strangers," Geo said, "but we'll never be that. We were important to each other." He looked away, then turned back and met Will's eyes. "I destroyed that. Of course you're angry with me—"

"Don't flatter yourself. I don't feel anything for you." Will's jaw worked. The struggle to contain his emotions was as obvious to Geo as a flashing neon sign.

"We can't change the past," Will continued. "There's nothing to discuss. We'll simply behave like two professionals. Are you capable of that?"

Geo smirked, but before he could respond, the conference room door opened. Suki stepped inside. Her shiny dark hair was shoulder length and cut at an angle, the look sophisticated. "The cars are waiting out front to take us to the restaurant," she said in a sunshiny voice.

Geo was happy for the respite.

The hostess led them to a private dining room decorated in a French provincial style. The walls were cream colored, the carved moldings painted gold. A crystal chandelier hung from the ceiling.

Geo made sure not to sit next to Will. He didn't trust himself. Nor did he want to make Will any more uncomfortable than he already was.

Still, it was a small group. They could hardly ignore each other during the entire meal. Small talk seemed to dominate the conversation. Geo knew how much Will hated that.

After they ordered, Will asked Oscar, "How did you come to found Crisanto?"

Oscar grew quiet a moment, his jaw tightening. Geo had never heard this story, but it didn't look like a happy one.

"I came up with the idea for the software at the last company I worked for," Oscar said. "I pitched it to my boss, and he seemed to like the idea. But then, he put the development budget toward one of my co-worker's projects."

He sipped his water, then continued, "I didn't think much of it at the time—her project was a sound investment. But then, a few months later, she and our boss got engaged. And I couldn't help wondering..." He just shook his head.

Geo arched his brows. The revelation explained a lot about how Oscar ran Crisanto. Most of his policies were forward-thinking, but he had a strong bias against employees dating. "That sucks," Geo said.

With a shrug, Oscar replied, "It worked out for the best. I quit my job and developed a basic version of the software on my own. With the profit from the sales, I brought on more developers, and we added more features. After a couple of years, business took off."

"You have a lot to be proud of," Will said.

"Thank you. I look forward to the opportunities for expansion that Pemberley offers."

The group grew quiet as the arugula salads were delivered. Geo was almost too amped up to eat, but he didn't want to let on anything to Oscar.

Will turned to Chanisse and said, "Tell me about your grandchildren."

She brightened, her usual quiet demeanor gone. "Desta is three, and Terrence is coming up on his first birthday. My daughter is planning a party. I offered to help, but she wants to do it on her own."

With that, the talk of business ended. Suki regaled them about her recent rock-climbing excursion with her brother. Oscar told stories about taking his wife and kids to visit his brother's winery just outside town. "They've got a guest house that looks out over the vineyard. The sunset views are gorgeous."

"I've always thought it would be fun to have a bed and breakfast," Suki said. "Meeting people from all over the world, making fancy scented soaps by hand—"

"Anyone can rent out a spare room to vacationers these days," Oscar said. "When you're ready to look for a house, you could get one with a rental suite. It's a good way to bring in extra cash."

The two of them were soon off and running, bouncing ideas off each other. It made Geo's head spin. He turned to Mandie, who was sitting between him and Will.

"Do you have any sightseeing planned while you're here?" he asked.

"Probably stay in the city, close to downtown," she said. "Seems like there's a lot to do."

"You mean Will hasn't got every minute of every day planned out for the two of you?"

She patted Will's back. "CEOs don't have time for sightseeing. He'll spend the weekend catching up on work."

A hot stab of jealousy shot through Geo at the way she touched Will. They were clearly more than co-workers. Had Will added women to his repertoire over the past ten years?

Will's posture straightened. "You sound like my last boyfriend," he said to her drily. "But I do manage to find *some* time for fun."

"Poor Will," she said in a teasing tone. "Your boyfriends always live down to your expectations."

Geo choked on a laugh. Because that described the Will he knew perfectly.

Will did not laugh. He gave her a chilly look.

"Oh, come on, just say it," Mandie urged. "You're dying to tell us how none of the men you've dated have been worthy of you. How difficult it is to find a man who isn't beneath you."

"That's not what I think, Melinda."

"Amanda," she reminded him.

Geo watched them, realizing they had fallen into some kind of banter that was typical of them. Jealousy flickered again. But her next words alleviated some of his discomfort.

"What were we talking about? Oh, yeah," she said, "I'm hoping my boyfriend will fly out for the weekend. What about you, Geo? Any fun weekend plans?"

"Unfortunately, I don't have a boyfriend at the moment," he said. "Or a girlfriend."

Will stiffened a moment but quickly regained his composure. His facial expression was one of studied indifference.

Geo struggled not to grin at that reaction. It meant something to Will that Geo was available. But could Geo break through his walls? Did he even want to?

The only thing he knew for sure was that he didn't want to lose this job. He'd only been at Crisanto a year, but it was the kind of place where he could build a career. No one gave him shit about being bisexual. No one treated him differently. The place felt like a family.

And Pemberley, it seemed, had the same sort of culture. Throughout the meal, Will showed a genuine interest in the personal lives of his coworkers. He made eye contact and smiled. Even cracked a joke or two.

Geo was impressed. As a young man, Will had done better one-on-one than in a group setting. But now, he seemed friendly and confident, even among people he had just met. He must have cultivated that skill at some point during the past decade.

Whenever his eyes met Geo's, though, his smile faded. His expression turned as cold and businesslike as Geo had ever seen it.

That stiff demeanor had fascinated Geo when they were younger. It was the face he showed the world, but not the side Geo usually saw. Geo saw the warmth and vulnerability.

But one mistake had cost him that right. Not that Geo could complain. He had made a choice, knowing what the consequences would be.

He'd told himself the risk was worth the reward. But he'd gambled and lost everything. If it hadn't been for the kindness of a stranger, he might have ended up on the street.

That act of grace had saved him. He'd gotten his addictions under control. He'd learned discipline in the military. He'd found his self-respect again.

But none of that mattered to Will. The man looked at him as if they were strangers.

After lunch, they walked the few blocks back to the office. The sunshine felt good on Geo's face, even if the temperatures were cool. Near the Convention Center, giant red Christmas ornaments roughly the size of Volkswagens decorated the lawn.

It was Texas, after all. Go big or go home.

Geo managed to fall into step with Will. "Lunch was fantastic. Thank you. I feel a little awkward, elbowing in like this."

"Think nothing of it."

Was that intended to be gracious, or was Will dismissing him again? Maybe a little of both. Will's coolness irked Geo.

No one seeing the two of them together would have guessed they had once been wildly in love. Geo still felt the spark between them. He wanted to explore it, even if it could never lead anywhere.

Although to be honest, he would be happy if they could just clear the air.

Gathering in the conference room again, the transition team discussed the upcoming all-hands meeting where they would announce the merger to the Crisanto employees. All the talk of "change management" made Geo's head spin. He was out of his depth.

Why was he even here? He'd served his purpose. The contracts had been signed. His presence made Will uncomfortable. He should back out now.

His mouth dry, Geo swallowed, then cleared his throat. "This part is all new to me. I'm not sure how much I can contribute at the meeting. I understand if you don't want me involved—"

"I want you involved," Will said abruptly. He didn't explain. He didn't have to. He was the CEO.

Was it an olive branch?

Will wasn't being a total prick. That was a surprise. Not so much because Will was putting business first— Geo expected that from him. But what did Geo have to offer that overrode the pain and distrust of the past?

The fact that Will still valued him—something about him, at least—meant the world to Geo. His throat grew tight. With an effort, he forced himself to focus his attention back on the meeting.

He didn't want to screw this up. Even though he was the person at Crisanto most likely to lose his job because of the merger. He was the least senior person in his department. A separate legal team at Crisanto was redundant. And his skills were specialized, so there wasn't another place for him in the company.

And he had gotten the CEO's baby sister drunk on her eighteenth birthday and tried to marry her for her trust fund in a quickie Vegas wedding.

Geo wasn't going to beat himself up over that again. Over the past decade, he'd done plenty of that. He wasn't the same man anymore.

Whatever the outcome of this merger, he cared about his coworkers. He wanted them to succeed. And maybe if he put everything he had into this exercise, he could prove to Will that he still had merit as an employee.

Even if his worth as a friend had been lost to the eroding forces of time, and to the worst mistake of his life.

Chapter 3

Will stood quietly at the front of the training room after the all-hands meeting. A few stragglers had stayed until almost five, asking questions. He had answered them honestly. Transparency was important to him. He hoped he had allayed their fears.

Despite some tense moments, the meeting had gone well. Some employees were worried about disruption to their jobs. Some were upset that Crisanto was losing its identity as a Latino-owned business. Will listened to their concerns and allayed their fears as best he could.

He hated public speaking every single time. Still, it was part of his role as CEO. It allowed him to control the corporate message. He was growing more comfortable at it, and better, too, he thought.

It had been the right call to include Geo in the presentation. During the panel discussion, the man had turned on the charm. Just as Will knew he would. With his wicked smile and self-deprecating humor, he had disarmed the audience.

Will had never met a more charming man than Geo. The quality made him irresistible. For most of his life, Will had had no reason to resist.

But what Geo had done to Will's sister had been unforgivable. Whatever mistakes Will had made, they didn't justify Geo's betrayal.

The memories ought to fill him with disgust. Instead, thoughts of Geo did unaccountable things to his groin. Geo was still the best-looking man Will had ever seen. But why should that matter, after all that had happened between them?

Will unclenched his jaw and swallowed hard. It would not do to let Geo distract him during this transition. It was too important.

Oscar and Mandie stood chatting. Will slung his computer bag over his arm and walked up beside them. Mandie turned to Will. "All set?" she asked.

"I have a question first. Do you two think Geo needs to be involved in the rest of the transition meetings? Earlier, he seemed to think he was redundant."

Will suspected Geo thought nothing of the sort. The offer had been a way to give Will an out. Either way, he intended to take it.

"I can handle it without him," Mandie said, "unless Oscar wants him there."

Oscar nodded thoughtfully a moment. "With Becca on leave, we could use Geo back at his regular job."

"Good. I'd like to be the one to tell him so, if you don't mind," Will said to Oscar.

The other man frowned but did not protest.

Will found Geo's office. The man was sitting at his desk staring into space, but rose when he saw Will. A smile swept across his face.

Will set his jaw, fighting the wave of desire that hit him like a punch to the gut. No one should be that attractive.

"You look exhausted," Geo said.

Will's brows rose. Whatever he had expected Geo to say, it wasn't that. He'd expected the man to be concerned about himself, not about Will. "I am, a bit."

"Come with me."

"Why?"

"Don't ask questions. Just trust me." Geo leaned in close and said in his ear, "I promise you'll like it." He smelled of soap, a fresh scent like the ocean. The feel of his breath on Will's skin twisted his insides into knots.

Reluctantly, Will followed him to a door just down the corridor. It opened onto a patio separated from the street by a hedge and shaded by tall trees. Just beyond the concrete landing was a Zen garden with a bench, a bamboo fountain, and raked gravel.

Will couldn't help it. He smiled. "This is lovely."

"Suki's idea. She's fantastic."

"She is," Will said tersely. "You should ask her out."

Geo chuckled. "Oscar has strict fraternization rules." His expression turned serious. "You impressed me today. A hundred-fifty people were afraid for their jobs, and you reassured them."

"You helped. With that Wickham charm, you put them at ease."

"Ah," Geo said with a nod. "That's why you wanted me there."

"Of course." Will saw the opening, and he took it, much as he hated to. "As for the rest of the transition meetings... Oscar thinks your time would be better served by going back to your regular duties."

Geo's lips flattened, and the shine dulled in his eyes. "Oscar does?"

Will gave a curt nod. "Mandie can handle it from here."

"Of course."

At Geo's cool tone, a wellspring of emotion rose in Will's chest. He wanted it to be anger or outrage, but it felt more like hurt. The one thing Geo had never been to him was aloof. "This isn't personal."

Geo let out a strangled laugh. "How can anything between us not be personal?"

Will's hands trembled. Geo was right—he was exhausted. He had been up since four. All he wanted now was food and a comfortable bed.

"For what it's worth," Will conceded, "I'm glad to see you're doing well."

Geo's lips parted as if the sentiment startled him. "Thank you. That means a lot."

Will looked out over the evergreen hedge at the tall buildings beyond. "I still don't trust you."

"I'd be shocked if you did."

The last light of the setting sun glimmered low in the sky, turning it a soft apricot. After a long moment, Will said, "If I could go back and do things differently..."

In a husky voice, Geo said, "Me, too."

Will turned toward the door. "I should get back. It'll be dark soon. Mandie's waiting for me to walk with her to the hotel."

"I'll show you out."

Will met Mandie at the receptionist's desk, and gave Geo a nod in parting. With luck, Will would barely see the man again during his visit. That was exactly what he wanted. Wasn't it?

Geo had mentioned at lunch that he was single. Why did the fact of it make Will's blood rush? It had been a while for him, but he wasn't about to hook up with Geo. Not for old time's sake. Not to chase away the sadness in his chest at the memories of their lost friendship. Not for the satisfaction of seeing Geo on his knees.

Although that last image wasn't doing anything to combat his desire.

George Wickham at thirty-two was as attractive as he'd been in college. Maybe more so. His body was trim and athletic, and his face wore a maturity that hadn't been there before. This was a man who had experienced the trials of life.

Will would not let that sway him. The trust between them could never be rebuilt. Even if Will's cock begged to differ.

As Will and Mandie approached the hotel, a sense of familiarity washed over him. He hadn't noticed it that morning, but then, he had been in too much of a rush to notice anything. Had he been here before?

He traveled so much, hotels all looked alike to him. Yet the feeling seemed stronger than that.

He and Mandie stopped at the check-in desk and got their keys. He looked around. The artwork, the stone tiles, the lighting fixtures, the seating areas. By the time they reached the elevator banks, he was sure. This wasn't his first visit.

Will had been to downtown Dallas only once before. That meant...

He steeled himself against the invading emotions. His assistant always booked him at the best hotel in town—just like his father before him. It wasn't surprising that it was the same one where he and Geo had stayed the weekend of the funeral. He should have considered that.

When they reached their floor, he and Mandie parted ways. He stepped into the executive suite. A flood of memories washed over him.

The gray-painted bookshelves, the teardrop chandelier, the floor-to-ceiling windows that showed off the skyline view. All conjured bittersweet emotions. The pain of losing Geo's dad was still sharp inside him.

The Wickhams had worked for the Darcy household, Geo's dad as major domo, his mom as housekeeper. For Will and his sister Ana, they had been surrogate parents, especially after the loss of their own mother. The Wickhams had lived in a cottage on the property just steps from the main house. Will and Geo had been inseparable growing up.

Once she was old enough, Ana had tagged along after them. She'd climbed up into their treehouse with her dolls, scaring Mrs. Wickham half to death. By the time she'd turned thirteen, it was clear Ana had a crush on Geo. Some part of Will had worried she'd steal Geo away from him. After all, Geo liked girls. He could never want Will the way Will wanted him.

But in this hotel suite, Will had learned how wrong he was.

He found the luggage in the sitting room. His checked bag was there, too—apparently the airline had found it. He wheeled the suitcases into the bedroom with the king-sized bed.

If he could avoid it, he wouldn't step foot inside the room with the two queens. The one where he and Geo had stayed. Where they had kissed the first time and made love the first time. No point making this situation harder than it was.

Will changed into jeans and ordered room service. Mandie would be joining Suki for a night on the town. Will, though, needed down time after a long day.

He answered a few emails and got ready for bed at nine. He'd been up since before dawn, after all. But his mind was churning. Seeing Geo again, being in this suite again—the memories crowded Will like a physical presence.

After lying in bed for a fruitless hour, he got up to make some chamomile tea. He placed a mug of water in the microwave. As he waited for it to heat, he tried to put Geo out of his mind to no avail.

The grief of losing his dad had wrecked eighteen-year-old Geo. The heart attack had been sudden and deadly. Will and his father had flown with Geo to Dallas for the burial.

Will's father suggested Will and Geo share a room at the hotel, so Geo wouldn't be alone. Will didn't hesitate, even though it would be torture. Will loved him so desperately, every moment spent with his best friend made his whole body ache.

The night after the funeral, Will woke to the sound of Geo's smothered sobs. He got into bed next to him and took him into his arms. There he stayed until the tears stopped and the kisses started.

Will hadn't told anyone he was gay, but Geo knew. And when their lips met for the first time, it was like an inferno. All that pent-up teenage lust found an outlet.

That night was just the beginning. Three years they had been together. It was the happiest time of Will's life. Even after a decade, Will hadn't forgotten the smell of him, the taste. None of his encounters in the intervening years had driven away the sense of rightness he'd found in Geo's arms.

Until Geo started making demands. His love of excess had outpaced his love for Will, and their future had unraveled.

The microwave beeped, and Will drank the tea in the master. It was the only room in the suite that didn't carry memories from their last visit. He didn't want to think about their friendship growing up, about the magic of falling in love. None of that mattered.

They had parted ways. It had been for the best. There was no going back now.

Still, his last thought as he drifted to sleep was of Geo's body beneath him, their mouths locked in a desperate kiss.

The ding of a text woke him at six the next morning. Blinking a few times, he picked up his phone. The message was from Mandie.

Food poisoning, it read. Then, a moment later, *Salad bars are of the devil.*

Sorry to hear it. Hope you're feeling better soon. Sure it wasn't too much wine? he teased.

Fuck you.

Seriously, who told her she could speak to him that way?

Stay in bed, he replied. *Geo can fill in.* Because, of course. The universe clearly had it in for him.

Thank you, she replied.

He added, *I'll contact the concierge. She'll keep you supplied with ice chips and sports drinks and whatever else you need.*

After he dressed and ate breakfast, he texted Oscar about the change in plans. Will didn't have Geo's phone number—what a disaster that might turn out to be. They would not be exchanging digits. When this trip ended, he would leave Geo behind forever.

All during the morning meetings, the awareness of Geo crawled beneath Will's skin. Geo was respectful and businesslike, yet Will could not stop thinking about how it felt to be inside him. How good it had been. How much he wanted to do it again.

Geo had been his first, so Will had assumed that sex would always be that way. That perfect melding of body, mind, and spirit. It was only after he lost Geo that he discovered how magical their relationship was.

In ten years, nothing else had come close.

Naturally Will wanted that again. But how could their relationship be the same, after the deception and betrayal? When Will thought of his little sister standing before the justice of the peace with a bridal bouquet in her hand and Geo at her side...

Instead of the old anger, he felt an awful hollowness in his chest. He had to distract himself, because the feeling was too much like longing. And that was madness. Despite the physical attraction, he could not possibly want Geo again.

At lunchtime, they went out to a Tex-Mex barbecue joint. Will sat as far from Geo as he could at the small table. Yet the whole time, he could feel Geo's eyes on him. It wasn't even intentional. Geo could no more ignore Will's presence than Will could ignore his. The pure animal magnetism between them was as powerful as ever.

On the way back to the office, Geo insisted they walk through Pioneer Plaza. Will didn't want to go. It was one of his most vivid memories from the last time they were in Dallas. The emotions it evoked were pure torture. But there was no graceful way to back out.

The park was several acres of lawn and low trees. A sculpture garden depicted a nineteenth century cattle drive. Dozens of larger-than-life-sized Longhorn cattle were cast in bronze, along with equally oversized cowboys on horseback. They crossed a shallow stream and ranged over limestone cliffs.

The last time Will had been there, Geo had talked of climbing onto the backs of one of the steers. He had seemed determined to do it—Will had grown angry and frustrated trying to convince him of the folly of such an idea. To this day, Will didn't know whether Geo had been serious or just baiting him.

Will wondered whether Geo would make the suggestion again. He did not. Apparently Geo was less reckless at thirty-two than he had been at eighteen.

"You've been here before, Will?" Oscar asked.

"Yes, on my last trip."

"Must have been memorable," Geo suggested with a sly smile.

"Quite," was Will's only reply.

Geo walked in step with him, slowing the pace until the others had outstripped them. "Remember that copse of trees?" He pointed with a lift of his chin.

Will answered matter-of-factly. "You told me you wouldn't climb onto the sculpture if I gave you a kiss."

Geo quirked his eyebrow as if daring him.

"It was a long time ago, Geo. Even if I were interested, which I'm not, this is not the time or place."

"I could come to your hotel room tonight."

Will's body heated, enough that his cheeks must surely have flushed pink. "That would not be a good idea."

"Just to talk, then."

Will knew perfectly well that if this man came to his hotel room alone for any reason, they would not just talk. "What would be the point?"

"To clear the air."

"We spoke yesterday. The air is cleared."

"There are still a thousand things I want to say to you."

Anger roiled up from Will's gut. "Geo, that part of our lives is behind us. We're business associates now." Regaining his composure, he added in a cool tone, "Best to keep it that way."

"Best for who? For you? So you can pretend you don't feel the pain of regret? I know you feel it, because it's eating *me* alive."

Sadness encompassed him. A dull ache lodged in his solar plexus and spread outward. He forced himself to say, "I've accepted that we're no longer part of each other's lives."

Geo scoffed. "Even if I never see you again, you will always be the most important person in my life." He walked faster, catching up with the others.

Will felt as if he were moving through molasses, his limbs heavy. Sorrow crushed his chest. Yet as his legs moved mechanically forward, a strange sensation rose from his belly. Something that felt surprisingly like hope.

Will could not still be in love with this man. How was that even possible? He would not let these misplaced emotions get the better of him.

Chapter 4

The next day, Mandie was feeling less queasy but exhausted. That meant another day's reprieve for Geo. The past forty-eight hours had been enough to convince him. Not only did he want to keep his job. He wanted Will.

The spark between them—it wasn't just a spark. It was an inferno. Will was trying valiantly to hide it. But Geo knew him.

Will was a wreck. A decade's worth of emotions were struggling to break free. When he finally let go, Geo wanted to be there.

When Will allowed himself to be vulnerable, he had a tender side as different from his stony CEO persona as it could be. Geo knew he'd have to work to win back Will's trust. Maybe it was too late, and he was kidding himself. But he had to try.

After morning meetings and a catered lunch, a teambuilding session was planned for the afternoon. They were painting murals for the children's wing at the local library.

The transition team laid out large sheets of heavy paper and pots of paint on the tabletops. The design was already in place, a sort of fairyland with trolls and princesses. It would be up to the employees to add the color according to a paint-by-numbers scheme.

They had put on old T-shirts brought from home over their business attire. Chanisse stood scowling, clearly feeling ridiculous. "I have some quarterly financials to work on. Maybe I could—"

"Relax, Chanisse," Geo said. "Have some fun."

"I think accounting is fun," she countered.

"Live a little," he urged.

She picked up a paintbrush, dipped it in white paint, and brushed a long stroke down the bridge of his nose. "You're right. That was fun."

Will laughed, and Geo looked over at him. "You think that's funny?"

"You look ridiculous."

"Do not tempt me." Geo picked up a cloth and wiped away the paint. It was water soluble, safe for children, so he wasn't worried. But he would get his revenge on Will before the day was over.

Some managers and HR reps joined the transition team. Each stood at a different table to lead the exercise. Then, at the top of the hour, the employees filed in.

Oscar explained the task, opening by talking about the partnership between the company and the library. Will said a few words about Pemberley's commitment to continuing Crisanto's work in the community. Then, as the painting got underway, Will walked from table to table, taking a few minutes to talk to the people at each one.

Geo watched him, making an effort to do so unobtrusively. Will was an imposing man, tall and broad-shouldered. In his shirt sleeves, with the cuffs rolled up, his normal formality softened. His baritone was smooth and confident but also kind.

Even from behind, Will was mesmerizing. His broad back, his slim waist, his perfect round ass. Geo wanted to strip every stitch of clothing off him and see his body in all its glory.

Geo had to stop thinking that way. He'd end up with a woody in front of the entire company if he didn't control himself. He focused his attention on the painting to distract himself. But his animal awareness of Will did not subside.

Finally, Will came to Geo's table. After a few minutes of chatting with the others, Will said to him, "Why are your apples yellow?"

Geo shrugged. "Sometimes apples are yellow."

"According to the numbering scheme, they're supposed to be red. You're interfering with the artist's vision." Will's voice was mocking.

"It's a children's mural," Geo pointed out. "I made the wagon red to balance it out."

Will's expression was stoic, but a laugh played in his eyes. "Do we need to have a conversation about following the rules?"

"I also colored outside the lines. Are you going to scold me about that, too?"

Will crossed his arms. "What kind of message does it send the children if you color outside the lines?"

Inwardly, Geo beamed at the attention. Outwardly, he matched Will's emotionless tone. "That it's okay to color outside the lines."

"You do realize that that sort of talk leads to the crumbling of society as we know it."

"Society as we know it could stand to lighten up." Geo dipped his brush into the red paint and drew on Will's cheek.

Some of the others at the table laughed, while some stared at Geo for his audacity. Will gave him a level look, but at least the stony expression from the first two days was gone.

The activity wrapped up around three o'clock, and by three thirty they had finished cleaning up. Geo sauntered back to his office to work. But that turned out to be a hopeless endeavor. He couldn't quell the hope that there might be a chance—however remote—of him and Will finding their way back to each other.

Geo's life might have turned out differently. Mr. Darcy—Will's father—had paid for Geo's college and left him money for law school. Money that Geo had squandered playing high-stakes poker in Atlantic City.

Geo had only meant to have a little fun. But the gambling and alcohol took over his life. As his bank account dwindled, he took more and more risks. Within a year, the money was gone.

So he did the only thing he knew how to do. He asked Will for more.

Will had been beyond pissed. They'd broken up shortly before Mr. Darcy's death, but had remained friends. Will had even gotten him into rehab, from which Geo had relapsed the day he got out. When Will learned the money was gone, he washed his hands of Geo.

"It's time for you to stand on your own feet," Will said. "If I keep coming to your rescue, you'll never take responsibility."

"You don't understand." Geo threaded his fingers through his hair, pushing it back from his forehead. "I have nothing to live on. I'm supposed to start law school at Penn in the fall, and I don't have the money for tuition."

"Then I guess law school will have to wait. In the meantime, I suggest you get a job. You've heard of those, haven't you?"

"Don't be a prick."

"In the past year, you wasted a small fortune on entertainment. Now you're asking for more. And I'm the one being a prick?"

"You inherited a billion dollars, Will. A half million is nothing to you."

Will's jaw tightened, his eyes growing hard as obsidian. "You're the one who treated a half million as if it were nothing. You spent it like water. Clean yourself up, and get a job. If you can live responsibly for three years, then I'll consider putting you through law school."

In retrospect, Geo realized, it had been a fair offer. Better than he deserved. At the time, he had felt alone and rejected. If Will wouldn't give him the money, he knew someone else who might.

And that was when Geo had done the irrevocable thing.

He had taken advantage of Ana, of the crush she had on him. He followed her to Vegas, where she had gone with friends to celebrate her birthday and high school graduation. She had already started on the champagne when he got there. Talking her into the quickie wedding was the easiest thing in the world.

But Will, the ever-protective brother, had followed her, too. Finding out from her drunk friends where the two of them had gone, Will stopped the ceremony just in time.

"He wants your trust fund," Will told her, his voice pleading, unable to even look at Geo. "He needs money for law school."

Ana turned to Geo, eyes unfocused. "No, he..."

But even in her inebriated state, she could see the truth in his expression. He couldn't keep up the pretense. His cheeks burned hot with shame.

She threw her bouquet into Geo's face. Then, she walked out on unsteady feet, her arm in Will's. That was the last time Geo had seen either of them.

Now he had a second chance. He wasn't that stupid kid anymore. Ten years was long enough to live with regret. It was time to put things right.

Geo stood at his desk, contemplating his next move, when the sound of determined footsteps caught his attention. Will barged into the office and scowled as he closed the door.

"You painted a heart on my cheek." Will sounded more bewildered than angry.

Geo quirked a half smile and lifted his brows. "Did I?"

"You know you did." Will pushed his hair back from his face. "How could you be so indiscreet?"

"How is that indiscreet?"

The furrows in Will's brow deepened. "You were flirting with me. Surely everyone who saw you do it must have realized that."

In truth, Geo hadn't consciously chosen a heart. He'd just acted. Will had looked adorable with that red heart painted on his cheek. Geo couldn't bring himself to regret it.

"I'm sorry," he said anyway. "I'll be more circumspect in the future."

"Please do. It would be awkward if anyone found out about our past."

Geo wasn't sure why that was. Aside from the fact that they'd pretended to meet for the first time on Monday. He wasn't sure why they'd done that.

Will had been shocked to see him, obviously. Geo had been somewhat prepared, having had two hours' notice. But the way Will had glared at him, it didn't appear he wanted to acknowledge the acquaintance. It had seemed more circumspect to pretend they were strangers.

Now, of course, it would be awkward to come clean. In ten more days, Will would be back in Philadelphia, and it wouldn't matter.

Geo's stomach wrenched. He couldn't bear the thought of letting Will go.

Not when Will was looking searchingly at him, emotions playing across his face. That heart had meant something to him. In his own oblique way—maybe without even realizing it—he was asking whether that heart had meant something to Geo, too.

Geo looked into those dark eyes, into the combination of confusion and hope and consternation that shone there. Hell, the man was handsome. Geo dropped his guard and said huskily, "I'm intensely tempted to kiss you right now."

Will stiffened and looked as if he might faint. His eyes widened and his face paled. Geo had to stifle a laugh at how easy it was to rattle him. Will put on a careful show of control, when inside, he was a wreck of emotions.

Geo couldn't help but be gratified at having that effect on him. He said in Will's ear, "Let me come to your room tonight."

Will shuddered. He didn't pull away. Geo held his breath, not pushing his advantage. He let Will adjust to the new emotional landscape.

Will tugged at the sleeve of Geo's jacket. Geo's knees nearly buckled at the power of that almost-touch. It was intimate yet so tentative. Geo's lips burned, his arms ached, but he held back.

Will's Adam's apple bobbed. "I'm having a reception in my suite for the transition team Friday night. You're invited."

Geo swallowed. It wasn't a proposition. It was an opening. Will probably didn't know his own intentions.

So Geo didn't ask him to put them into words. Instead, he said, "What time should I be there?"

Will licked his lips. "It starts at seven."

Geo's cock jumped. He would be there at six.

Chapter 5

Will looked into the mirror in the bathroom of his hotel suite. Some remnants of the heart remained on his cheek. Even though he had washed off the paint in the men's room almost as soon as Geo had put it there.

And maddeningly, Will liked that Geo's mark was still on him. That Geo had laid claim to Will's body. After all these years, that physical desire had not abated.

He had been avoiding examining those feelings for three days. But in this place, in this hotel room, he couldn't escape the memories of Geo. Of the love they had shared. Of the past that was every bit as real to him as the present.

Will changed into jeans and stepped out into the sitting room. Sorrow permeated him. The remnants of loss were imprinted on this space.

He had loved Geo's dad. And Geo had been destroyed. Losing both his parents by the age of eighteen had flattened him.

It was a pain Will had learned for himself three years later, when his own father passed away. That time, though, he and Geo had grieved separately. Their affair had crashed and burned a few months before.

What if Will had put aside his pride and sought Geo's comfort? Could they have repaired their relationship? Could the heartache of the past ten years have been avoided?

Will put those thoughts aside and walked down the hall to check on Mandie. She greeted him wearing boots and a cowboy hat. He laughed. "Been shopping, have you?"

"Just in the gift shop. After being cooped up here for two days, I was getting a little stir crazy."

"Your color looks much better than it did yesterday."

Her eyes sparkled, another positive sign. "A good night's sleep, and I should be back to normal."

He smiled. "Glad to hear it. I talked to the concierge. She's sending up an assortment of soups and breads for you to try for dinner."

"That's sweet of you."

Her words warmed him. He wanted to hug her. But should he?

She had been sick, and was probably craving comfort. But even though they were friends, he was still her boss. A hug seemed...

He didn't know what it seemed. He was terrible at social graces. When he had been dating Geo, Will had relied on him for that. Will had never quite figured it out on his own.

He compromised, putting his hand on Mandie's shoulder. "I'm relieved you're feeling better."

"Me, too. Did I miss anything important?"

He shrugged. "Geo's been handling things. I believe he sent you his notes from the meetings?"

"Yes, I checked my email. Everything seems to be progressing on schedule."

"I'm a little worried about Crisanto's head of operations. He seems committed to doing things his way. He keeps using words like *regulation* and *certification* to argue about why we can't change anything."

She grinned. "Did you mention that you were chief operating officer at Pemberley before you became

CEO? So you already know all about regulations and certifications?"

"Not yet. I want to give him time to adjust to the takeover."

She nodded. "You're a good guy, Will."

"Not really. If he continues to resist me, I'll win and he'll lose. That's a foregone conclusion. It's easy to be gracious when I don't have anything at stake."

A knock came on the door, and a redhead from room service set up the food on the dining table. After giving her a generous tip as she departed, Will turned to Mandie. "Would you like some company for dinner?"

"Please. I'll never finish all this alone."

They ate and chatted a while. Then Will raised a question he had been meaning to ask her. "Geo mentioned something to me about Crisanto's fraternization policy."

"Ah yes, that." She stirred a bowl of chicken soap with thick noodles. "Becca warned me about that. She's been trying to change it for years, but Oscar is emotionally invested. You heard the story he told Monday."

"Is it something we should be concerned about?"

She considered a moment. "I'd put it under the heading of pressing, but not urgent. With everything else we've got going on, it's not a priority. But it's on the list."

Will nodded pensively.

She grinned at him. "So does this mean you're thinking of asking out someone from Crisanto?"

Will sat up straight. "What?"

"Please. I saw the way you were checking out Geo's ass. Can't say I blame you. That man is *fine*."

"I don't know what..." He let his voice trail off. Because he knew exactly what she was talking about. It was a terrible habit, the way he stared when his brain fixated on something. He didn't even know he was doing it. Apparently his brain had fixated on Geo.

"I thought you were practically engaged," he deflected, drawing attention from the heat in his face that must surely show as a deep blush.

"Yes, but my eyes are fully functioning. I can enjoy the view, even if I don't want to handle the goods."

Will had to change the subject. He was getting aroused just thinking about handling the goods.

"I'm teasing," she said. "The man is a smooth operator. You're too smart to fall for someone with that much charm."

And Will was also too smart to fall a second time for a man who had betrayed him.

At least, CEO Will was. But that guy was apparently back in Philadelphia. The Will in Dallas was eighteen again and yearning for his best friend.

He needed to summon CEO Will, and fast.

Mandie seemed to tire, so Will let her rest. Back in his room, he tried to catch up on email. In his role, it was critical to make quick decisions and move on, something he was good at. Tonight, though, his mind would not settle.

He walked to the floor-to-ceiling windows in the sitting room. The panorama of skyscrapers was spectacular. Buildings were lit up in green and gold, silhouetted against the dark sky.

He felt Geo's presence beside him. Some part of his brain must have conjured that memory. It wasn't a picture, just a sensation. A feeling of intense sorrow, but also of rightness that they were together.

Together as they had always been. Until Geo had given him that ultimatum, and everything had fallen apart.

At the time, Will had been furious. How dared Geo try to force his hand? In retrospect, though, Geo had been right. If Will had done what Geo wanted, would they still be together now?

He had asked himself that question many times over the years. It was as if his life had followed two parallel paths: what was, and what should have been.

Will had expected to go through the rest of his life feeling that way. As if half of him was missing. As if he was living a paler version of the life he should have led. Now, he had a second chance. Would he take it? Or did the wounds run too deep?

After that last, horrible betrayal, Will didn't know if he could ever trust Geo again. He only knew one thing for sure: he wasn't ready to say no yet. He wanted to try.

Chapter 6

The next morning, Mandie returned to work. Geo didn't attend the day's meetings. But Suki invited him to join them for the catered lunch.

When Geo first met Suki, he'd considered asking her out. She had seemed to return his interest. But Crisanto had a zero tolerance policy when it came to employees dating each other.

Geo had talked to Becca, his boss, about updating the fraternization policy to something more in line with industry standards. Oscar wouldn't hear of it. Geo had been disappointed—Suki was lively, pretty, and smart—but he wasn't about to get himself fired over her. Oscar adored her in a sort of fatherly way. There was zero wiggle room there.

So now Geo felt kind of shitty, taking advantage of her soft spot for him to finagle a lunch invitation. But damn it, he had nine days to win back Will's heart. He would work every angle he could find.

Geo would not let Will get away again.

As Geo entered the conference room, basil and garlic spiced the air. He filled his plate with baked ziti and Caesar salad. Without hesitating, he sat down next to Will.

The man gave him a level look, but there was amusement in his eyes. Will didn't like games. Geo was making it perfectly clear what he wanted.

"Mandie, how are you feeling?" Geo asked.

"Better." She sipped her water. "But no more salad bars for me."

"Glad you're okay," he said. "I emailed you some more updates. I'll have the trademark list for you by the end of the day."

She nodded. "Good. We won't decide for a while about changing the corporate entity on the registrations." She gave Oscar a reassuring smile before turning her gaze back to Geo. "But Pemberley might want to license a few in the meantime."

"Sure," Geo said with a smile.

He had a good feeling about Mandie. She was easy to work with. Also, she was kind of a smartass. She gave Will the kick in the butt he so often needed.

More importantly, she looked after him.

Geo wasn't the best at caring for his own emotions. But Will was on a whole other plane, the way he compartmentalized and closed himself off. The only time he expressed his emotions was during sex.

It sounded as if he hadn't been with anyone for a while—at least no one he cared about enough to let his guard down. It was good he had a friend he could be himself with.

More than that, though, Will looked like he was starved for touch. As if he was so brittle, he might shatter from a slight breeze. Geo remembered their first time together, how Will had trembled, how that touch was everything. And Geo had needed it, too.

Geo wanted that intimacy back. Not just Will's love and friendship, although that was just as important. He wanted the freedom to wrap the man in his arms when he looked the way he did now. As if the pressure of the world's expectations was crushing him.

In the end, though, it was Will who made the first move. Mandie asked for a list of HR policies that had been discussed in the previous days' meetings. Will said, "My man Geo can get you that," and patted Geo's back.

Heat suffused his whole body from Will's touch. Could Geo be blushing?

He didn't want anyone to see evidence of the attraction between him and Will. So he got up, dropped his plate in the trash, and went for dessert.

Suki had ordered the mini-cannoli that Geo liked. Taking a couple, he sat back down. He offered one to Will.

"I wish I could," Will said. "I'm stuffed."

"No, seriously, you have to try this." Geo held it out, and Will took a bite. "Am I right?" Geo asked. "Is that not the best thing you've ever put in your mouth?"

Holding Geo's gaze, Will licked a bit of cheese filling from his upper lip suggestively.

A choked cough came from across the table. Mandie was watching them with wide eyes, her face screwed up as if holding back a laugh. Her cheeks pinked as she looked down the length of the table. Oscar, Chanisse, and Suki were locked in their own conversation, oblivious.

"Excuse me," Mandie said, and fled the room.

Geo looked at Will deeply and feigned a serious tone. "Do you think she's scarred for life?"

"She'll be fine, once she composes herself."

"What are you going to tell her?"

Will looked at him innocently. "About what?"

In low tones, Geo said, "About us."

Will put on his stiff and formal expression, but his eyes still danced. "There is no *us*, Geo. You're imagining things, poor man. I understand how irresistible I am—"

"You're full of shit."

Mandie rejoined them and gave them a stern glance. It was not one to be argued with. And she was right, they were behaving recklessly. Geo hadn't meant anything suggestive about the cannoli, but...damn. That had been hot.

The team took a break after lunch. The Crisanto employees went back to their desks, while Will and Mandie stayed in the conference room catching up on email. Geo wasn't quite ready to get back to work, so he stayed.

He wondered whether he was making Will uncomfortable, though. The guy had grown tense again after Mandie's silent rebuke. "You look like you could use a massage," Geo said to him.

Will looked up, eyes wide. His gaze swept toward Mandie, then back to Geo. He seemed to be saying *not in front of her*. But he did not seem to be saying no.

In fact, if Geo was going to do this, it would be best to do it in front of the woman who happened to be Pemberley's chief legal counsel as well as Will's best friend. That way, nothing inappropriate could happen.

Geo rose and stepped toward him.

Will looked at him like a gazelle who had caught sight of a predator. "You don't mean to—"

"Relax," Geo purred, and the fight left Will. He clearly didn't want to have this conversation in front of Mandie.

Geo shut the door. He walked up behind Will, hands trembling as he rested them on those broad shoulders. Geo swallowed to clear the emotion in his throat, so thick he could scarcely breathe. His heart thudded painfully, as if his chest weren't big enough to hold it.

The feel of Will's warmth under his palms sent a rush of electricity through him. He gently pressed his fingertips into that hard muscle. Will kept typing, but his pace slowed. He relaxed into Geo's touch.

Mandie looked askance at them. "What is this flirty-flirty thing going on here?" Her scowl deepened. "Geo, did they teach you about sexual harassment in law school, or were you sick that day?"

Without taking his eyes off Will, Geo said, "It's only harassment if it's unwanted."

She narrowed her eyes at him, then turned to her boss. "Will, are you okay? You look uncomfortable."

"He's uncomfortable because he likes it," Geo said. "He just doesn't want to admit it. If he wanted me to stop, he'd tell me so."

Will didn't flinch as he quipped, "Geo thinks that if I sleep with him, I won't be able to fire him."

Geo laughed aloud at that. "I'm not that devious."

"Of course you are."

"Okay, I am, but that's not what I was thinking."

"Then let's prove it," Will said in a voice that did not brook argument. "Mandie, draw up a contract that says I can fire him even if I fuck him."

Geo's hands stilled. Mandie's wide-eyed expression settled into a scowl. "If that's what you want," she said.

"I want the contract," Will clarified.

"Fine by me." Geo's thumbs kneaded the muscles of Will's neck. They were rock solid, but his skin was soft and warm. Geo wanted to lean over and breathe Will's scent. "All I want is for you to relax. You've been tense since you got here four days ago."

"He's been tense as long as I've known him," Mandie said.

"Then stop riding my ass," Geo complained.

Will chuckled.

"Okay, I've had enough." Mandie closed her laptop. "I'm getting out of here. You two behave yourselves. Or at least lock the freaking door." She took her computer and mouse, and closed the door behind her.

Geo worked his fingers upward and massaged Will's scalp. Will let out a soft moan. It was the same sort of sound he made when Geo's mouth found Will's cock. Geo had missed that sound.

"Let me come to your hotel tonight," Geo said in Will's ear.

"I won't let you into my hotel room until I've got a signed contract."

"You want to put me on my knees and threaten to fire me if I'm not a good boy."

Will let out a groan, and Geo chuckled. His dick was fully hard now, and he was sure Will's was, too. Teasing Will like this was torture, but he had the man where he wanted him.

Almost.

What had Mandie been thinking, leaving the two of them alone together? Geo had to go. What he really needed was a cold shower, but some distance between them would have to do for now.

Geo kissed Will's crown, then headed back to his office. He closed his door and leaned against it. His body vibrated with desire.

This was happening. Will wanted him, at least physically. Was it possible that a fling between them could lead to more?

The fact that they worked together was a complication. Not that Geo would let that get in his way. As much as he loved this job, he'd give it up happily for a chance to be with Will again.

He opened his computer to video chat with Becca, his boss. She was still in Florida. But he had some questions only she could answer.

"Hey, Becca," he greeted when she came on the screen. Her auburn hair was straighter than she usually wore it. Her makeup was more casual. But her expression was as serene as ever. As if, no matter how bad things got, they'd find a way through.

"How's your mom?" he asked, turning on the charm.

Becca shook her head. "She finally agreed to an assisted living facility. She can't stay in her own home, and she refuses to move back to Dallas..." Becca pursed her lips. "Anyway, it'll be a few weeks yet. We're looking at places, and they all have waiting lists."

"Good luck. I hope she's recovering okay."

"She is. We're lucky she didn't break a hip or anything. What's up?"

"There's something I need to check with you," Geo said. "I've been working with HR to harmonize our corporate policies with Pemberley's. Most of them are pretty close, surprisingly. Family leave, anti-discrimination... But as you can imagine, the fraternization policies are very different."

She nodded. "I doubt Oscar will budge on that. I've tried, believe me. Unless Pemberley pressures us to change it, I think the Crisanto policy needs to stay in place."

Geo pursed his lips. He hated being sly about this, especially with Becca. She'd been good to him. But at this point, he couldn't afford to give anything away. He was too vulnerable.

"In that case," he said, getting to the real reason for the phone call, "we need to clarify something. What if a

Crisanto employee wants to date a Pemberley employee?"

Becca raised her brows. "Good question. I'd need to check the wording, but I think the Crisanto policy only applies if two Crisanto employees are dating each other. Otherwise, the Pemberley policy would apply."

"That's how I'm reading it, too. I'll run it by Mandie to see what she thinks."

"Be sure to involve HR in any discussions," Becca urged. "And don't make a final decision without consulting me."

"Will do." Geo bit back a laugh. More like, *do Will.*

Geo ended the call, feeling hopeful for the first time in a long while. Maybe this could work. Maybe this time, Will could finally be his.

Chapter 1

Mandie handed Will the contract the next day, as soon as they were alone together in the conference room. "I represent Pemberley Industries in this," she reminded him. "I suggest you get your personal lawyer to look it over. I advised Geo to do the same."

From her tone, it was clear to Will that she was pissed.

"Thanks, Mandie. I understand this was difficult for you."

"I don't get it," she said. "Speaking to you as a friend, that is. Geo is a player. I know you can see that."

Will considered that a moment. "I don't know that he's a player. He's manipulative, certainly."

"And you're going to let him manipulate you."

He grinned at the double entendre. "I haven't decided yet."

She rolled her eyes. "Why? I mean, I get that it would be convenient to have a booty call whenever you visit Dallas..." She shook her head. "Is that what this is?"

"I don't know yet what it is. Maybe it's nothing."

She gave him a hard look. "I don't trust his motives."

"There are things about the situation you don't know."

She eyed him assessingly. "Fair enough. And I suppose you don't want to tell me."

He looked at her softly. "It's complicated. No need for you to get involved any further than you already are."

She scoffed. "If you say so."

"Let me know when you get the signed contract from him."

"Of course." She rose and left the room.

Will sighed. She was upset—or so he thought. In truth, Will understood neither women nor emotions, so he could never be sure. He hated the idea of upsetting her, though. She deserved better.

Maybe he ought to confide in her. But what good would that do? She would tell him what Geo did was unforgiveable. But Will wasn't prepared to throw away twenty-two years of friendship because of one day.

And yet, that's exactly what he *had* done. Geo had been struggling with grief and addiction, and he had made a terrible choice. After ten years, Will finally had enough distance to put it into perspective.

Will contacted his lawyer. The man didn't object to anything in the contract. Will signed it and handed it to Mandie that afternoon.

She made a copy, giving it to him along with Geo's signed copy. "You are now free to move about the cabin," she quipped.

"I wish you weren't upset about this."

"I wish I weren't, too." She crossed her arms and glared at him. "This is going to blow up in your face."

"What if it doesn't? What if it's the best thing that ever happens to me?"

She arched her brows skeptically. "You think George Wickham might be the best thing that ever happens to you?"

"I do."

Her face fell. "Oh, honey." She came over and hugged him. "I hope, for your sake, that it works out. But if it doesn't, I will be there to help you pick up the pieces."

He let himself linger a moment. She was warm and soft in his arms, and she smelled like peaches. But her breasts were pressed against him, and that was awkward. He pulled away. "Thank you, Mandie. You're a good friend. I probably don't say that enough."

"Or ever." She giggled, an un-corporate-lawyer-like sound.

That evening after work, Will got ready for the reception. He showered and dressed in khakis and a blue Oxford shirt with the sleeves rolled up.

He checked the clock on the bedside table. It was five forty-five. The food would be delivered around six fifteen, and the guests would start arriving around six forty-five. So he opened up his computer to work on a report he wanted to finish before Monday.

He had not been working long when a knock came on the door to the suite. It might be the food, a little early. But he hoped it was someone else. His heart beat rapidly as he made his way to the door.

He looked through the peephole. It wasn't the food. He took a few deep breaths to steel himself.

He opened the door. "You're early," he said to Geo. A golf shirt showed off his thick biceps. His artfully unruly curls begged Will's fingers to run through them. Will's mouth went dry at the thought of kissing that chiseled jaw, rough with a hint of stubble.

The man strolled in as if he'd been invited. "Do you mind?"

Will did not respond, just closed the door and watched his old friend.

As Geo looked around, his smirk quickly faded. The expression was replaced by one of shock. "This is the room!" he cried, turning to Will, his eyes wide, his mouth twisted.

"It is."

"And you've been staying in here for four days?"

"Of course."

Geo stared as if Will had grown a horn in the middle of his forehead. "Why didn't you ask to be moved?"

Will scowled. "Because this is the best room in the hotel."

Geo covered his face with his hands. "Holy mother of..." Straightening, he met Will's eyes. "I don't think it's good for you to stay in this room. Too many sad memories."

"Good memories, too, though." Will swallowed. "The best thing that ever happened to me happened here."

Geo eyed him for a long time but said nothing. Then he walked over to a silver-framed mirror that hung above the gray-painted credenza.

"I remember standing in front of this mirror," Geo said, "trying to tie my tie for my dad's funeral. I couldn't get my hands to work." He turned to face Will. "You tied it for me. It was the worst day of my life, but you made it bearable."

In two strides, Will crossed the room and pressed his mouth to Geo's lips, soft but firm beneath his. His body had acted before he knew what he intended. His mind would not have gone along with the impulse. But now, Geo was in his arms, devouring him like a man starving.

The feel of that strong, muscled body against him was like oxygen to a drowning man. Like sunshine wakening the leaves of spring. Like a missing puzzle piece falling into place.

Despite the time and hurt between them, this felt right. The smell and taste of Geo were familiar. Their mouths fit perfectly together.

Will's hands explored him, wanting more, more, more. Geo was as fit now as he had been at twenty. Will's hands slid beneath Geo's knit shirt, fingers brushing against hard abs and soft skin.

With his blood rushing to his cock, the thinking part of Will's brain turned off. He didn't care about tomorrow or ten years ago. Right now, in this moment, he wanted Geo naked. They had time. What he had in mind wouldn't take long.

It took a moment for him to register the knocking at the door. He pulled back to see Geo's eyes glazed and heavy-lidded, as his own must be. *Damn it.* Could someone else be here already?

His brain slowly rousing, he walked over and looked through the peephole. A young Black woman in a ponytail and a crisp suit stood with a catering cart beside her. Will smiled and sighed in relief. "Room service," he said to Geo, who gave him a wry grin.

The two men helped her set up dinner in the bar area. Nothing perishable—not after Mandie's experience. "Would you like me to uncork the wine," she asked, "so it has a chance to breathe?"

"Please," Will said. Once she had gone, he locked the deadbolt behind her. He turned and looked at Geo, unsure what to do next.

But Geo knew. He walked up to Will and deftly unbuttoned the blue Oxford. Will leaned back against the door, unsure he could remain standing otherwise. So many emotions. It was too much.

Geo pressed kisses along the curve of Will's neck. Behind his closed eyelids, Will saw lightning bolts. "Bed?" Geo asked.

Will drew him in for a deep kiss. Then, he took Geo's hand and led him into the master suite.

This was possibly the worst idea he had ever had, but he could not make himself care. His cock was calling the shots now. None of his other lovers could compare to Geo, and his body wanted to feel that sweetness again.

He took off his shirt and carefully laid it on the bed. Geo, meanwhile, had tossed his shirt into a crumpled heap atop the bedspread.

Their bodies slammed together. As their mouths met, they teased and sucked and nipped. Will trailed kisses along Geo's shoulder, leaving a mark. He wanted Geo to have reminders on his body for days.

He danced Geo into the bathroom. Will wet a washcloth and left it on top of the vanity. When he turned around, Geo's jeans and briefs were already pooled at his feet. Will sucked in a breath at the sight. The next moment, he fisted that hard, thick cock, and Geo gasped.

Geo fumbled with Will's belt while Will pumped him. Their lips met again in sloppy kisses. The cool air hit Will's body as Geo pushed down Will's khakis and boxers. Then, Geo's hand was on him.

Will let out a groan that seemed to come from the deepest recesses of his lungs. All his breath rushed out of him. He grabbed Geo's ass in one hand and fit their cocks together in the other.

It was pure bliss, so good he knew it would end before he was ready. Geo grabbed some lotion from the vanity to ease the friction. The smooth glide of their pricks together made Will's heart race and his blood hum.

"Hell, I've missed this," Geo said.

"Who gave you permission to speak?" Will asked.

Geo chuckled and hauled him in for a kiss. One hand held Will's nape while the other found his nipple. A low groan caught in Will's throat.

Geo rocked against him, speeding up the rhythm. "Fuck, that's good," Geo said. "I won't last."

"Don't come until I do."

Geo groaned at that. But Will's dominance was all for show. He was desperate. He wouldn't last, either.

Deep kisses engulfed his senses. The taste was achingly familiar. Why had he given this up? He had been a fool.

Geo's lips moved to an earlobe, and Will caught a glimpse of them in the mirror. That was all it took. He came long and hard, cum spilling over his hand.

Geo quickly followed, Will's name on his lips. Will kissed him while reaching for the washcloth. It was cool to the touch as he cleaned them up.

"Holy shit." Geo buried his forehead in Will's neck. "I forgot how good that was with you."

"I didn't," Will rasped. "I remember everything."

They stood there holding each other, catching their breath. Then, Will checked his watch. He pulled back, and Geo moaned in protest.

Will gave him an apologetic kiss. They dressed quickly. It was six thirty, and the others might start arriving at any moment.

As they walked through the bedroom, Will said, "Stay with me tonight." It came out as more command than question. "If you want, I mean. It's not a condition of employment."

Geo laughed at him, a happy sound. His blue-green eyes sparkled.

Embarrassed, Will ran his fingers through the short-cropped hair at his nape.

Geo stalked up to him and pressed his hands to Will's chest. "I'd love to stay."

Will's stomach did a somersault. He shouldn't want this, but he did. He wasn't going to question that. After all, he'd only be in Dallas for another week. They'd get this out of their systems and move on.

Right? This wasn't their future. This was now. And Will intended to make the most of it.

Chapter 8

Usually Geo liked his coworkers. At the moment, he wished they would all go the hell home.

Ian from HR was chatting with Karen from IT. Geo had fantasized about the two of them more than once, both separately and together. Ian was slim but athletic, a ginger with a trim waist and round ass. Karen was a geeky brunette with a great rack and a booty that wouldn't stop.

Now, Geo couldn't believe he'd been attracted to either one of them, while Will Darcy existed in the world.

The man was a god. An Adonis. A perfect specimen of manhood. Right now, all Geo could think about was experiencing that manhood in its full glory.

Didn't these people have families?

Geo walked over to where Will was standing at the bar. Geo dropped some ice cubes into a glass with a clink, then filled it with seltzer water. In low tones, he said, "Can't you get rid of these people?"

Will's laugh was a low rumble. "Patience, my friend."

"You know me. That was never my strong suit."

"We've got all night."

"Fine. I'll mingle."

Will gave him an affectionate smile. "You're good at mingling."

"I'm distracted."

Will drew his brow. "Go talk to Mandie. She's been glaring at you all night."

"She's protective."

"She is." Will's voice deepened. "She thinks you'll break my heart."

"Maybe you'll break mine."

Will eyed him for a beat. "Talk to her."

Geo went over and took her by the hand. Without a word, he led her into the master bedroom and closed the door behind him. Standing in front of the picture windows, the cityscape beyond, he said, "Out with it."

"I don't know what you mean." Her tone was clipped.

"You want to yell at me, so yell at me."

She narrowed her gaze. "If you hurt him, I won't just see you fired. I'll see you disbarred."

"Fair enough."

That answer seemed to piss her off. Apparently, she wanted a fight. "I don't know what your game is. I'm sick for two days, and I come back to work to find you trying to get inside the CEO's pants."

"Do you think I'm trying to steal your job, Mandie? Because I'm not."

She stiffened. "That never crossed my mind." She threw her hands up. "Fuck! You're trying to steal my job."

"Why is it so hard to believe that I'm simply attracted to him? That maybe I wouldn't mind a transfer to Philadelphia so we can be together?"

She gaped, her eyes widening. "You've known him since Monday. It's now Friday. And you're already talking about moving halfway across the country for him? It's his money, isn't it. You want his money."

Geo couldn't be offended by that. After all, there had been a time when he *had* wanted Will's money. "Have you ever been in love, Mandie?"

"Of course." She scowled and crossed her arms protectively. "My almost-fiancé is flying here to see me tomorrow. He had to postpone his flight because of a family thing, so he won't be here until the evening... But what does that have to do with you and Will?"

"When you met your almost-fiancé, did you know he was The One?"

She let out a thin stream of air. "He had a girlfriend at the time. I wanted to scratch her eyes out."

"Because some part of you knew he was yours." Geo gave her a gentle smile.

"I guess?"

"That's how I felt when I saw Will on Monday. I knew if I let him get away, I would regret it for the rest of my life."

She narrowed her brow. "You're a smooth talker, aren't you."

"I'm not bullshitting you. I have no ulterior motive. I want Will."

She closed her eyes and massaged her temples. "Please don't hurt him," she said softly.

"I'll do my best. I take it you've seen him hurt before."

"You have no idea," she said with fire in her tone.

"Tell me."

She paced around the room, gesturing with her hands. "It's always the same. He's rich and he's hot, and guys want to be with him. Then they find out he's difficult and closed off emotionally, and they don't like that as much."

She broke off a moment before continuing. "But by then, they've gotten accustomed to the lifestyle he offers. They don't want to end it. They think they can have their cake and eat it to. But Will knows. He's not a dumb guy. And every time, it hurts him a little more."

She met Geo's eyes beseechingly, then shook her head. "I can't believe I told you that."

"I'm glad you did." He stepped closer. "It helps me understand the things he might be sensitive about. But Mandie, I love the fact that he's difficult and emotionally aloof. It's a façade, you know. It's just a matter of getting behind it and reaching the real Will."

She gazed at him deeply. "How can you possibly know that after four days?"

Geo swirled the ice in his glass. "He reminds me of someone I used to know."

She pursed her lips, still wary, but seemed willing to let it go at that.

They rejoined the party. The crowd had thinned a bit. Mandie took off, still tiring easily after her illness.

Others soon followed. There was a line for the powder room. To speed things up, Geo led a couple of people to the bath in the second bedroom. The one with the two queen beds. It didn't look as if Will had used it at all since checking in.

In the dim light, after the others had gone, Geo stood at the window looking out over the city. Memories of the last time he had been in this room washed over him. He missed his dad. And his mom. The past ten years had been hard without them.

The army had been his family for a while. Then, when he started law school, he came to Dallas and reconnected with his aunts and cousins. That had been a welcome change. Still, he had missed Will and Ana. They had been the most important part of his childhood.

Will stepped into the doorway. "There you are. Anyone else still here?"

"No, just me. Anyone else left out there?"

"Not a one." He pursed his lips. "It's not a good idea for you to be in here."

"Like you said, there are good memories here, too." Geo sat on the bed, the one where they had...

Will sat beside him. "It's easier to cope with the memories with you here."

Geo leaned in and kissed his cheek. "Whatever you need, Will. Let me give you what you need."

Will squeezed his hand. "Did you clear the air with Mandie?"

"I don't know." Geo shrugged. "She doesn't trust me. I guess time will tell. If I don't break your heart, maybe she'll accept that I'm not the world's most terrible human."

"No," Will said, his voice tight. "You're not that."

"You must have thought I was, at one point."

Will looked down at where his hand was joined with Geo's. "No. But you ripped my heart out. I always thought we'd get back together, but then you tried to marry my sister."

His words rocked Geo to his core. "You wanted to get back together?"

"Of course."

Of course? Geo had felt utterly rejected. He had never dreamed Will still wanted him. "Even after the gambling?"

"You were addicted. I didn't know how to fix it. I thought tough love..."

Will's voice grew tight. "The day you got out of rehab, I should have moved you in with me so I could keep an eye on you. I was so angry with myself that I didn't do that, after you relapsed. You didn't need tough love. You needed unconditional love."

Geo's voice escaped as a whisper. "I thought you were disgusted with me."

Will's thumb stroked the back of Geo's hand. "I've never been good at parsing my emotions. My heart was broken. That's all I can say."

Geo laid his head on Will's shoulder. Will kissed his temple. "I made so many mistakes."

"How can you say that?" Geo asked. "It was my fault—"

"If I had come out when you asked me to, we'd still be together now."

The words barreled over Geo. For so long, he'd blamed himself for everything. Now, it seemed like Will was offering him absolution, at least for some of it. It felt like a reprieve from a death sentence. He tried to speak, but the words caught in his throat.

Will continued, "If I weren't so stubborn, we'd be married now. Maybe have a baby or two. I don't know why I was so adamant about keeping us a secret. Why I thought my father would care that I'm gay. I was a dumb kid, Geo. And it cost me the person I cared about most in the world."

Geo's eyes burned. He straddled Will and found his mouth. They lost themselves in deep, scorching kisses. Will's palms grazed over Geo's back, keeping him close.

A sense of release washed over Geo. Will didn't blame him. It seemed like a miracle. Geo pressed a kiss to Will's cheekbone and nipped his ear.

"We should anoint this bed," Geo said. "Again."

Will groaned, the sound gruff and needy. "The supplies are in the other room."

Geo gave him a lopsided grin. "We can use spit."

Will arched his brows, giving him a scolding look. "We're not going to use spit when I've got perfectly good lube in the other room."

"Fine." Geo sighed long-sufferingly. "We'll do it your way."

"Of course we will." The corner of Will's mouth quirked up. "Have you forgotten who you're talking to?"

Geo laughed. "So bossy."

"You love it."

"I do," Geo said. "And I love you." The words flowed from him before he had a chance to think about them. He held his breath.

Will nuzzled him. "I never stopped loving you."

They dissolved into long, breathless kisses. Geo was painfully aroused, but he didn't want to rush this. He'd dreamed of this night for so long, he wanted to enjoy every moment of it. Every tantalizing glide of tongue against tongue, every brush of palm over heated skin, every panting moan of pleasure.

Before long, Geo was rutting against Will, their cocks sliding together. The heat of passion left him fevered, his brain turning to jelly. He wanted to meld into Will. To erase any separation between them.

"Need you," Will said, mouth gliding along the rim of Geo's ear. "If we don't go to the other room now, I won't be able to stop."

They rose and walked hand in hand. Geo waited as Will stood in the middle of the room, to let Will take control if he wanted. But Will hesitated. Geo suspected he felt too much. That he was overwhelmed.

Once Will got started, he would be fine. His body would take over. Geo knew that from past experience. Right now, though, Will was too much in his head.

Geo took off his shirt, then unbuttoned Will's. That got Will's muscles working. He pulled at Geo's belt, unbuckling it, then unzipping his fly. He nipped at Geo's neck while pushing his jeans and briefs down toward the floor.

Will grasped at Geo's ass cheeks with those big, warm hands. "Mine," Will said. "No one else's."

"Only yours," Geo said.

They stripped down, and Will guided Geo to the bed. Geo was soon on his back while Will got the supplies from the nightstand. "How long has it been for you?" Will asked softly.

"A while."

"Then we'll take our time." Will worshipped Geo's body with kisses, from the hollow of his throat to the dusky peaks of his nipples to the tender insides of his elbows. Geo knew to relax and enjoy, rather than reciprocate. Another time. Right now, Will was in charge.

As Will's mouth followed the trail from Geo's navel to his groin, Geo's cock jumped. The desire was so intense, he thought it might swamp him, drowning him in the pervading ache.

The tip of Will's tongue teased the slit, and Geo gasped. Licking down the shaft to the seam of Geo's balls, Will traced circles around them. Then, Will dipped further, teasing his taint, and Geo groaned.

Geo fisted the sheets, wanting to come but not wanting this to end. When was the last time a lover had taken this much care with him? Made him feel so desired and loved? He couldn't remember. Maybe not since the last time with Will.

He ran his fingers through Will's hair. "You're so good to me."

Will kissed the juncture of his thigh and groin. "I've missed being good to you."

"I don't deserve it."

"Don't say that." Will glided his thumb worshipfully up and down Geo's shaft. "You were the best friend I've ever had. That hasn't changed."

"For me, either."

"Then relax and enjoy this."

Geo nodded and lay back. He refocused his attention on Will's ministrations. The sensations were warm and teasing. Will seemed to remember exactly what Geo liked. After three years together, they had known each other's bodies as intimately as their own. Maybe even more so. Now, it was as if no time had passed at all.

Will glided his tongue back up Geo's cock and took just the head in his mouth, meeting Geo's eyes as he did so. It was intimate and commanding and hot as fuck. There was nothing submissive about the way Will sucked cock. You always knew you were at his mercy.

Will took him deep, and Geo's body bucked. Hell, that was good. Hot and wet and perfect. But Will wasn't done with him yet.

He got out the lube and glided a finger across Geo's hole while he laved his prick. It wasn't enough suction to make him come, just enough to keep him on edge while slick fingers worked him open.

When the pressure hit Geo's sweet spot, shivers rushed over him. "That's it," he cried.

Will grinned smugly. "Did you doubt me?" For emphasis, he stroked the spot again.

It had been so long, and Geo missed this sensation. This closeness. No one else had ever made him feel the way Will did. His touch was insistent and sure. He gave Geo exactly what he needed.

It would be easy to fall into the myth of forever. To believe Will would always want him the way he did now. Geo wouldn't go there. He would take each moment as it came, enjoy this while it lasted. Because nothing in his life made him feel as good as loving Will.

"Now," Geo said.

"Are you sure you're ready?"

"Ready to explode."

Will kissed his way up Geo's abs to his nipples. He rolled the sensitive tips between his lips, then lightly flicked with his tongue. Geo rode wave after wave of pleasure, never reaching the crest, writhing and shuddering under his lover's ministrations.

Will pressed a kiss to Geo's lips. His eyes were glazed with desire, as Geo's surely were. "Please," Geo murmured.

Wordlessly, Will suited up and found Geo's entrance. With their gazes locked, Will pressed inside just enough to breach him. Geo gasped at the stretch.

Will pulled back. "Tell me if I hurt you."

"It's okay if you hurt me."

"Geo," he scolded, "I'm a man of considerable size. I can't do this if you won't be honest with me."

"Yes, sir." Geo's whole body lit up with that evidence of Will's care and concern. He drew Will in for a kiss, tender yet passionate.

Will thrust in again, deeper this time, sliding against Geo's prostate. The burn grew into a sweet ache of pleasure, the intensity enveloping him, driving him closer to the edge.

Geo canted his hips up, taking him deeper. But Will wouldn't let him fall over, wouldn't give him that last frenzied burst of pleasure. "Slow down," Will said. "We have all night."

Geo whimpered, but Will ignored the protest. Instead, he fucked him at a leisurely pace, their eyes still watching each other. Will's expression was serious and determined, as if prolonging each moment of pleasure was a critical task that required all his concentration.

Geo kissed him, their mouths molding together. Their bodies found a happy rhythm. He never wanted it to end.

Will's eyelids fell shut and the muscles of his face softened, as if his control was giving way. "Hell, you're tight."

"You think so?" With a wicked grin, Geo clenched his muscles and thrust up, taking all of him.

Will swore, fighting to regain control of the situation.

But it was too late. The urgency built to a frenzied pace. Will rose up and grabbed Geo's cock, pounding into him and fisting his cock at the same time. Geo came with a shout, shuddering as waves of cum shot out of him.

Will rode him hard now, keeping nothing back. He cried out as he let himself go, pouring everything he had into Geo. Then, he collapsed on top of him, breathing heavily. "Mine," he said, nipping Geo's ear.

And just like that, Geo was as much in love as he had ever been. He buried his face in Will's neck, fighting back tears. Nothing in his life had ever felt so perfect, so natural.

He was Will's. Always had been, really. And he didn't know whether he could survive losing him a second time.

Chapter 9

Will lay on his back in the darkness, Geo's head resting on his chest. He pressed kiss after kiss to Geo's temple, cherishing this moment. Will had had a few partners in the past decade. But he hadn't made love since the last time he was with Geo.

With other men, sex had been an enjoyable interlude. A release of tension. It had not been this emotion in his chest threatening to burst out of him. This whispering in his ear that said *forever*.

After all that had passed between them, was forever possible? He didn't see how.

And yet, he could not bear to let this man go. Not again.

He would never know true happiness if he did. He would be a shadow drifting through the corridors of what might have been. They had been in love once. They could be in love again.

He drifted off to sleep and didn't wake until dawn. His eyes fluttered open to see Geo watching him. With a smile, Geo brushed his fingers through Will's hair.

"I never thought I'd get to wake up next to you again," Geo said.

Will clasped Geo's hand and kissed the knuckles. Words could not capture what was in his heart, so he said nothing. Instead, he wrapped Geo in his arms and held him close.

They drifted off again until the sound of room service delivering breakfast in the sitting room woke them. "I smell coffee," Geo said without opening his eyes.

"Are you hungry?"

"I could eat."

They got up and put on hotel robes before going out to where the food was set up on the bar. Besides coffee and an assortment of teas, there was a bowl of mixed fruit, some hardboiled eggs, and a platter of pastries.

"Chocolate mini-muffins!" Geo smiled like a kid. "I remember these." He popped one into his mouth.

"When I told them last night I might have a guest, I asked them to send up some extra muffins this morning."

"You remembered?" Geo asked.

"I told you, I remember everything."

Geo kissed him, tasting like sugar and chocolate.

As they sat down to breakfast, Geo said, "Do you have any plans for the day? We could do something fun."

"I should work this morning. But maybe this afternoon."

Geo looked as if he wanted to scold him, but he refrained. "How about the aquarium?"

The suggestion reminded Will of the times he and Geo had gone diving in the Caribbean during their breaks from college. Once on St. Croix, they had surfaced to find a few dolphins swimming near the boat. He and Geo had hung out for a quarter of an hour watching them play, getting out of the water only when their air had dropped to a few hundred psi. It had been one of the most magical experiences of Will's life.

Will thought about how much of their lives he and Geo had shared. It was impossible to remember his childhood or his college years without thinking of Geo. Those memories had been tinged with sadness for the past decade. Now, he could recapture the joy again, if he let himself.

So Will agreed to Geo's suggestion. It would be fun to do something whimsical and touristy. He rarely had the chance for that.

In truth, he didn't have time today, either. But he wasn't married to this job. He deserved a day for himself.

Will worked for a few hours while Geo went home for a change of clothes. Geo came back to the hotel room carrying a gym bag. Will hoped that meant he planned to spend the night again.

Weirdly, Will realized, he hadn't meant sex when he'd had that thought. Of course sex was high on the list of things he wanted to do that day. But he wanted to hold Geo in his arms like he had the night before, to wake up with the man beside him again.

Was he growing attached too quickly?

He didn't have a plan, which was disconcerting. Will always had a plan *and* a contingency. Unlike Geo, he wasn't comfortable playing it by ear. But he couldn't predict where this would lead.

Geo came over to him and raised his brow. "Still working?"

"Not anymore." Will set his computer to hibernate. Rising, he drew Geo in for a kiss. It was soft and sweet, the passion subdued. They had time. No need to rush into sex again like a couple of teenagers.

Around one o'clock, they walked the few blocks to the aquarium, stopping for a late lunch on the way. The day was cool and clear. "It's nice to be out together like this," he said to Geo as they left the restaurant, "almost as if it's a date."

"Uh, dude," Geo said, "this *is* a date."

Will's steps stuttered a moment before he regained his footing. Geo was right, of course. "We'll have to be circumspect. Mandie said something about going shopping with Suki today."

Geo's face reddened. "Ashamed to be seen with me?"

"Not at all," Will said fervently, seeking to reassure him. "I have no desire to hide this relationship. Aren't you concerned about Oscar finding out?"

Geo nodded thoughtfully. "You're right. For now, as far as the world is concerned, we're just business associates."

Will hated the sorrowful undertone in Geo's voice. "I'm sorry. It's not like when we were in college. You work under me—"

Will broke off when a grin spread over Geo's face. "I could get on top," Geo offered.

"You know what I mean."

Geo nodded thoughtfully. "We'll make an announcement when the time is right. Until then, we'll have to keep it under wraps. Assuming we keep seeing each other. We haven't talked much about that."

"We will, though."

His words were met with a soft smile.

They reached the aquarium. Inside, they walked through the darkened corridors, close to each other but not touching. It reminded Will of their college days. They had been careful not to give anything away back then. Everyone saw them as best friends, roommates, nothing more.

Will hadn't minded. The sexual tension that built up inside them in public would explode when they were alone together. But Geo had hated the secrecy. He was a more physically affectionate person. Pretending to be friends had been hard on him.

Will should have been more considerate, more aware. He was the one with the money, the status. That put him in a position of power. He didn't recognize it at the time. But later, after the breakup, he realized that Geo hadn't always asked for what he wanted. And Will had not taken care of him as he should have.

This time around, he would do better.

They walked at a leisurely pace, stopping to look at exhibits of clownfish and moon jellies and spider crabs. When they got to the garden eels, Geo said, "I think these are my favorite."

"They *are* rather phallic looking."

"Is that what you think of me?" Geo murmured in his ear. "That I'm obsessed with sex?"

Will led him into a darkened corner. "I hope so, at least."

They stood close enough that Will could feel the heat radiating off Geo's body. The tension between them crackled. Will's lips ached to kiss him, his hands to glide down his sides and rest on his narrow hips.

"I'm disappointed in you, Mr. CEO. I thought you wanted me for my mind."

"I have a signed contract that says I can use your body anytime I want—"

"That's not what it says," Geo said sardonically.

"Close enough." Will reached for Geo's hand. But Geo stiffened and pulled away, looking over Will's shoulder.

Will turned to see Mandie and Suki approaching. *Shit*. He should not have been so indiscreet. In the dim light, Suki's eyes registered surprise, and maybe a little hurt.

If she told Oscar that Will and Geo were dating, it could create all kinds of trouble. And Will would have no one to blame but himself.

"Hey Suki," Geo purred, his voice smooth as silk. Will tensed at the tone. He had never heard Geo use it with anyone but him. But then, Geo might have used it with dozens of lovers in the intervening years since he and Will had been together.

Hot jealousy burned in Will's gut as Geo flirted with Suki. Had the two of them ever had a fling? Crisanto's policy forbade it, but Geo wasn't exactly one to follow the rules if he disagreed with them.

Will realized Mandie's eyes were on him, and he schooled his expression. He forced himself to speak to her as if everything were normal.

"Did you two go shopping?" he asked.

"We did, but I didn't find anything good. I wanted to get something special for Jared. Apparently it's stormy in Philadelphia, and his flight was delayed. He won't land until about eight. Which means we won't even have twenty-four hours together before he has to go home again."

Will squeezed her hands. He hated the forlorn look on her face. "I'm sorry."

"It's not your fault."

"It is, actually," he said with a crooked grin. "I'm the one who insisted on meeting face-to-face. You'd be teleconferencing from Philly if it weren't for me."

"You're right." She smiled, but then her expression turned sad again. "I can't help thinking that if he really wanted to see me, he'd have come last night."

Will scowled. "I thought some sort of family thing came up."

"It did. And he put that ahead of me. Because I'm not family. We've been dating three years, and he hasn't proposed."

He squinted at her. "Didn't you spend the first two years saying you didn't want to get married?"

"I did," she conceded, and let out a sigh. "I was an idiot."

"Maybe you should propose to him."

She shrugged. "It would force the issue, at least. I guess I'm better off finding out sooner rather than later."

He hugged her. "I'm sorry."

She gave him a squeeze before pulling back. "It's possible I'm making something out of nothing. He treats me like a princess, always has. But I'm thirty-four years old. High-risk pregnancy is a thing. If he's not ready to seal the deal, then I need to find someone who is."

Will thought a moment. "Has his flight left?"

She narrowed her brow. "Not yet."

"Then call him. You'll feel better if you hear the sound of his voice."

She eyed him sideways. "That's surprisingly good advice, coming from you." She took out her cell phone, gave him a smile, and stepped out of the exhibit into the bright corridor.

Will turned his attention back to Geo and Suki. He wished he hadn't. She was standing with her back to the wall. Geo was standing close and leaning toward her.

Anyone who didn't know better would think they were a couple. Or at least that he was making his move.

Was Geo into her? If that was the case, then why be so obvious in front of Will? Was he trying to make Will jealous?

Geo looked over and met Will's eyes. "What do you think about meeting Suki and Mandie when the aquarium closes," he asked, "and going to dinner at the steakhouse nearby?"

"Fine with me," Will said. He wanted to break something.

Mandie rejoined them, in a better mood. The foursome firmed up their plans. The women went toward the rainforest exhibit, the men toward the African. "Sorry about that," Geo murmured once they were out of hearing distance.

"About what?" Will asked in a sharp tone.

Geo chuckled. "Dude, I'm not interested in Suki. I was distracting her in case she saw something. She and Oscar are close. We have to be careful around her."

Will accepted that explanation, but an irrational jealousy lingered. "Maybe we should tell Oscar about us."

"Yeah, no, he would fire me on the spot."

Will startled at that. "Then you could move back to Philly with me."

Geo stopped short. "Is that what you want?"

Will couldn't meet his eyes. "I don't know what I want."

Geo said nothing for a while. "We need to have this conversation—soon."

"It hasn't even been twenty-four hours."

"Depends on how you count. I've been trying to win you over since Monday morning." Geo arched his brows enticingly.

"We can't do this here."

"You're right," Geo conceded, then gave him a bright grin. "Let's go find the penguins."

His lighthearted demeanor chased away any lingering fears. Will relaxed and enjoyed himself. But when they rejoined the women at five o'clock, the insecurities came back.

They sat in a booth, tan cushions and blond wood. Will slid in beside Mandie, and Geo beside Suki. Will met Geo's eyes across the table, telescoping frustration in his direction. Geo's expression told him to lighten up.

Instead, Will brushed his knees against Geo's beneath the table. The man let out a soft gasp. The contact made Will instantly hard. He suspected Geo was similarly affected.

"Should we order a bottle of wine?" Mandie asked.

"I think we'd better not," Will replied.

"It's fine," Geo said. "Don't let me stop you."

"You don't drink, Geo?" Mandie asked. Then, her face reddened. "Sorry, I shouldn't have asked that."

"No, it's fine. I don't mind talking about it. I've been sober for ten years, five months, and...seventeen days. Opioid blockers saved my life."

Will's mouth went dry. He did the math. Geo hadn't had a drink since Ana's eighteenth birthday. Since the last time Will had seen him.

Suki, sitting beside Geo, stroked his arm soothingly. "I interviewed him about it for our company newsletter. It was a series for mental health week. Oscar has worked to destigmatize mental illness so people will get the treatment they need."

Mandie nodded. "Glad to hear it. It's good for employees, and it's good for business."

"Geo was so open about his experiences, it touched a lot of people," Suki said, still stroking his arm. Will shot hand grenades at her with his eyes.

Suki was gorgeous with her smooth black hair, dark eyes, and flawless golden complexion. She was Will's opposite in every way. Outgoing, enthusiastic, warm, funny, light-hearted. All words that could describe Geo as well.

Was it any wonder he liked her company? Did Will have any chance of competing?

The only advantages Will offered were money and status. Geo liked those things well enough. But they were not exactly the qualities Will hoped would win him over.

Plus, she knew about Geo's life during the past ten years. About the things Will should know but didn't, because Will had abandoned him. A knot tightened in his stomach, stealing his appetite.

He ordered a bowl of tomato bisque soup and some Texas toast. If he were hungry later, he could add a salad when the entrees came. Mandie didn't look any happier than Will felt. "Are you okay?" he asked her.

"I think Jared is keeping something from me. The last couple of times we've talked, he's been evasive."

"You'll feel better once you see him."

"I suppose."

They turned their attention to Suki, who was talking a mile a minute. "Oscar's kids are so cute," she said to Will. "You'll see when we go to the winery tomorrow."

Oscar had invited them to tour his brother's winery. It was about an hour outside the city. Will was looking forward to seeing the vineyard, even though the vines would be dormant at this time of year. After a week in the city, he was ready for the wide open spaces.

Needing to move his muscles, he got up and went to the men's room. Geo came in as Will was washing his hands. "Tell me what's wrong," Geo said. "Is it Suki? Because there's nothing between us, I promise you."

"She knows what happened after Ana and I walked away. And I don't."

"We'll talk about it tonight."

"I should have been there."

"No, you shouldn't. Your job was to protect your sister from a predator, which is what you did. Maybe you've forgotten, but I haven't."

Will's body ached. He didn't want to think about this anymore. He wanted to go back in time ten years and five months and seventeen days, and make it not happen.

He'd tried life without Geo, and that hadn't worked out so well. But how could they get past all their mistakes, and make a life together?

He went back to the table, and Geo rejoined them a few minutes later. Even Suki's bubbly personality couldn't raise the mood. Will's stomach eased enough for him to order a chicken Caesar salad, though. For dessert, they split a couple of slices of cheesecake.

They walked Suki to her car, then headed to the hotel. The night was dark but streetlamps lit the city.

Mandie was still quiet—too quiet. Will put his arm around her. "What's wrong?"

"I think Jared and I are going to break up," she said, and started to cry.

Will and Geo cocooned her in a hug, right there in the middle of the sidewalk. Will marveled at how natural it felt. A week ago, he wouldn't have considered it. Even though she was definitely his best friend.

"If Jared wanted to break up with you," Will said, "he wouldn't fly halfway across the country to do it."

"He's keeping something from me."

"Maybe it's a good something," Geo suggested. "Maybe it's a surprise."

She pulled out of their embrace and dried her eyes. "I suppose it could be. I miss him so much. I was disappointed when he postponed his flight. I guess I got a little emotional."

"Nothing wrong with that," Geo said.

They walked into the lobby, Will's arm still around her shoulder. They were headed to the elevators when she stopped short. "Jared?"

She rushed over to the check-in desk and flung herself into his arms. He twirled her around, then gave her a fervent kiss. Jared was a big guy, even more so than Will, about six-five with broad shoulders. His hair was chestnut brown, and he wore a perpetual smile. He was beaming now.

"I thought your flight didn't get here until eight," Mandie gushed.

"No, I meant I'd be at the hotel around eight. But things didn't take as long as I expected, so here I am. Didn't you get my text when I landed?"

She took out her phone. "Battery must have died."

"You always forget to charge it when you travel."

"Anything breaks my routine, and I turn into a dumb blonde."

He chucked his finger under her chin and looked into her eyes. "You are never dumb," he said, and kissed her.

He looked over at Will. "Sorry, we're acting like a couple of schoolkids. Will, it's good to see you." He walked over and shook Will's hand.

"You, too." Will introduced Geo. Then, Jared headed back to the desk with a glowing Mandie in tow, while Will and Geo went to the elevator.

As the doors closed, Geo said, "That dude is in love," sounding surprised.

"I would say so."

"If I were a betting man—which I'm not," Geo said pointedly, "I'd bet you ten bucks he proposes tonight."

Will's brows narrowed. "Do you think so?"

"That's probably what he's been keeping from her."

"I hope that's it."

The doors opened, and they headed to the room. Once inside, Geo drew him into a kiss. "I've been wanting to do that all day," Geo said, and kissed him more urgently.

Will held him close, drinking in the comfort and desire of those demanding lips. But sadness lingered in his chest.

Geo pulled back. "Relax, dude. You're so tense."

"Possibly."

Geo combed his fingers through Will's hair. "Is this about Suki, still?"

"Possibly."

"Come sit down." Geo led him to the couch. They sat, and Geo pressed soft kisses to his cheeks and forehead. "We have so little time. Let's not waste any of it. Talk to me. Do you think I'm interested in Suki?"

"Not exactly. You're not a cheater. The whole time we dated, I never worried about you looking at someone else."

"So why now?"

Will shrugged. "Because you tried to marry my sister." His throat tightened. "You were standing with her at the altar of an all-night chapel when I got there. Literally moments away from saying your vows."

Geo nodded slowly. After a few moments, he said in a soft voice, "It wouldn't have been legal. We were both intoxicated. Quickie Las Vegas weddings are routinely followed by quickie Las Vegas divorces."

"But you would have slept with her."

Geo gaped. He jumped up and paced about the room. "Is that what you thought all this time? That I actually intended to sleep with her? Dude, *no*. She was like my sister." He gave a little shudder.

Will's head swam. He wasn't sure what to do with this new information. "Then why?"

"For the divorce settlement. I figured you'd throw a hundred grand at me to sign the papers without a fight."

That made more sense to Will, based on what he knew of Geo. Somehow the idea that it had been solely about the money was comforting. But could he trust anything Geo said about that night?

Geo's shoulders slumped. "I realize how awful it sounds. I used your baby sister and maybe broke her heart a little. I violated my own principles. But I would not have slept with her."

Will said in a strangled voice, "How am I supposed to believe that?"

Geo sat on the other side of the couch. "You either believe it or you don't. Anyone would think you were crazy to trust me after what I did. But it was one day out of twenty-two years of friendship. I was an addict, and I was desperate."

"That's no excuse."

"It's an explanation. I could not be more sorry, Will. I've suffered for it every day since. And either you find a way to accept that and get past it, or we go our separate ways."

Anger pulsed through Will. "Is that another ultimatum?"

"No," Geo insisted. "But I won't spend the rest of my life being reminded on a regular basis of the worst thing I ever did. It was a long time ago. If you can't get past it, then there's no future for us."

Will nodded. He sat in silence for a long time. Then, he rose and went into the bedroom, closing and locking the door behind him.

Chapter 10

Geo looked around the empty room, unsure what to do next. Fortunately, he knew Will. If Will wanted him to leave, he'd say so.

So Geo waited. He rose and looked out the window, watching the city lights twinkle.

Will had a lot to sort through. This was the big moment. If Will couldn't forgive him, it was over. Geo couldn't finesse this.

He had betrayed Will with Ana. But he hadn't slept with her. Did that count for anything?

For all these years, Will had thought Geo intended to do that. Geo shouldn't be surprised, even though the thought had never crossed his mind. Geo had seen it as a financial transaction, not a marriage.

What a selfish bastard he had been. Ana had idolized him. She'd loved him and trusted him and looked up to him. And with one supremely egotistical act, he'd destroyed that.

His heart hurt. He'd loved Ana, too. He'd have done everything in his power to protect her from a bastard like him. But in the end, he hadn't been worthy of her friendship.

What would she think of him and Will getting back together now? Did she even know they'd been a couple? She hadn't known at the time. They'd told no one.

And as far as Geo knew, they still hadn't. He hadn't, at least. Mandie was the only living soul who knew about their relationship, but even she didn't know about their past.

The old anger welled up inside him, breaking through his self-recriminations. If Will had just agreed to come out, none of this would have happened. But then, Geo shouldn't have pressured him.

He understood now that everyone had to come out in their own time. But at twenty-one, he hadn't understood. He'd thought it was about him—that Will was ashamed of him.

Will came from a prominent family, while Geo was nobody. That knowledge had colored every interaction between them. It took years for Geo to realize that maybe Will hadn't seen it the way Geo had. That maybe Will didn't care that Geo's parents had worked for Will's parents. That maybe Will had just loved Geo for who he was.

And Geo had fucked it all up. Why was he even here? There was zero chance that Will would be able to forgive him, not in the long run. Geo was good enough to fuck, but not good enough to marry.

He picked up his gym bag where he'd left it by the door. He turned the knob. Then stopped.

This was his last chance. His last chance for a future with Will.

As Geo lay on his deathbed, this was the moment he'd remember as the worst mistake of his life. Not that day in Vegas. This one. Because he had the opportunity to fix things but lacked the courage to try.

He let the door latch click back into place. Setting down his bag, he approached the master bedroom and knocked. The sound of footfalls approached, and Will let him in. Will looked sadder than Geo had ever seen him.

Now was not the time for talking. Geo cupped Will's face in his hands. Will did not resist.

The kisses Geo placed on Will's lips were tender and teasing. He did not rush. He gave Will time to respond to the comfort of his touch, to allow the heartache to ease and the passion to rise.

And rise it did. Will's kisses turned scorching and urgent as he drew Geo hard against him. Their hands worked frantically as their clothes fell to the floor, and Geo fell to his knees. He knew what Will needed from him.

Geo offered himself with loving submission. Stroking the trunks of Will's thighs, he reached one hand around and cupped that perfect apple ass. He kneaded it with his fingers, loving the resistance of firm muscle.

With his other hand, he guided Will's cock to his mouth. His tongue circled the head, then his lips glided over the shaft.

Will fisted Geo's hair and took control. "Mine," he growled.

There was nothing gentle about what came next. That long, beautiful cock was hot and thick as Will thrust with a rhythm of his own. Geo did his best to keep up.

"Take it all, dirty boy," Will ordered.

Geo couldn't respond, because Will's dick was in his throat. He swallowed, massaging it with his muscles. Will groaned. "Fuck, that's good."

He pistoned into Geo with punishing strokes. Slick with spit, the steely shaft massaged his tongue and soft palate. Geo offered no protest or resistance.

"That's it," Will murmured, tightening his grip on Geo's hair. "Good boy."

The praise sent a flush of warmth through Geo's system. Being used like this, knowing he was giving

Will pleasure, made him hard to aching. He wanted to touch himself but would wait until Will gave him permission.

Will said nothing, just moaned and gasped his mounting pleasure. With a sudden shout, he filled Geo with his sweet cum, goosebumps rising on his skin. Geo licked and swallowed as Will softened and then pulled out. It took a moment for their breathing to return to normal.

At last, Will knelt beside him, kissing him tenderly—hot, wet, greedy kisses. "I'm sorry," Will said.

"Don't be," Geo soothed. "I like it that way—I've told you that."

Will's hand found Geo's prick, sending tingles rushing through him. Will smiled. "Apparently you do. Lie back on the floor."

Geo obeyed, and Will's mouth worshipped Geo's body. He started at the jawline, then moved to the curve of his neck. Geo shivered at the sensations—the clinging lips, the teasing tongue. Next came a trail along his clavicle and down his breastbone, detouring to his nipples. Will laved and sucked until Geo was writhing beneath him.

Geo threaded his fingers through his lover's hair, murmuring encouragement, caressing his nape. Geo's cock was full to bursting. "Please, Will. Need you."

Will tongued his way down to Geo's navel, circling there before going lower still. He blew teasing breaths onto the cockhead before licking the ridge. Geo's hips bucked at the pleasure of it.

"That's it. More. Please."

But Will took his time. He suckled the cap, heating Geo's body. The anticipation prickled his skin. Finally, Will went deeper, lips sliding down the shaft.

Geo gasped. "Hell," he said on an exhale. "You're the king at that."

"Only the king?" Will teased.

"The emperor. The master of the mother-fucking universe."

Will's chuckle vibrated on Geo's cock. "The master of you, at least."

Geo shuddered as that wicked tongue continued to tease him. "My master," he murmured. "Mine."

With long, slow strokes, Will hollowed his cheeks. The pleasure was so sharp, so intense, Geo wanted it to last forever but knew he was close.

As if reading his mind, Will slowed his pace. He kneaded Geo's balls, then put his mouth there, enveloping them in his heat. Alternating from one to the other, he kissed and sucked. Then he found Geo's taint, and licked long strokes over the delicate skin.

All the while, Geo moaned in desperation. "You're killing me."

"Hush, naughty boy. You'll come when I say you can."

"Bastard."

Will shot him a grin. He fisted Geo's shaft, keeping him on the edge without taking him over. Geo murmured and begged, unable to form words.

Finally, Will took Geo's cock into his mouth again, stroking and sucking him. The orgasm hit hard and fast. Geo's mind blanked as he cried out, his body warming as if bathed in golden sunlight.

When the shuddering stopped, Will pulled him into an embrace, Geo's head resting on Will's chest. "Only you," Geo said, his voice raspy but laced with affection. "Only you could make me feel that way. No one knows me like you do."

Will caressed Geo's thigh and hipbone. "How did I live without you all this time? You're like oxygen to me."

A lump formed in Geo's throat. "I know what I did was unforgivable. Do you think you could forgive me anyway?"

Will raised himself up on one elbow and gazed into Geo's eyes. He ran a fingertip down the bridge of Geo's nose, down his lips and chin and Adam's apple. "I think I already have."

Tears pricked Geo's eyes. "How?"

"That's what you do when you love someone. When they make mistakes, you forgive them, and they forgive you in their turn. None of us is blameless in this life. I'm certainly not."

Geo took Will's hand and kissed the palm, too overwhelmed to speak, emotion clogging his throat.

"I want you close to me," Will said. "I can't stand the idea of leaving you behind when I go back to Pennsylvania."

Geo thrilled at the words. He didn't even mind the unspoken assumption that he would be the one to move so they could be together. It was a sacrifice Geo was willing to make. "We'll work something out."

"The legal team in Philly doesn't have an opening," Will said. "Maybe you could stay with Crisanto, working in Dallas while I'm traveling, and in Philly when I'm not. It's the best I can offer right now."

"I'll think about it." Geo wasn't crazy about the idea. Still, if it was for the short term, he could handle it. "It would give us a chance to figure this out before we commit to anything permanent."

Will's mouth hardened. "Of course."

"What?" Geo asked. "Did I say something wrong?"

"No, you're being practical. I'm acting as if we're back in college again. But we're not, and who knows if we're still compatible."

Geo sat up. He hadn't meant to imply that they might be unsuited now. "I don't think either of us have changed that much. Our circumstances have, that's all."

Will nodded pensively.

Another thought came to Geo, and tension gripped his stomach. "What about Ana? What will she think about this? Does she even know about us?"

Will hesitated a moment. "This floor is damned uncomfortable. Let's get in the bed."

"Okay." Geo hoped he wasn't trying to change the subject, because they needed to talk about this.

Geo lay on his stomach, pulling one of the king-sized pillows under his chest and leaning his arms on it. "If we get back together, will it cause problems between you and your sister?"

"She'll be pissed I never told her about us. Other than that, I don't think it will be a problem. She'd have contacted you years ago if I hadn't asked her not to. She checks up on you on Facebook. Tells me what's going on in your life. Didn't mention anything about you moving to Dallas, though."

Geo's heart swelled. "She doesn't hate me?"

"I don't think she ever hated you. She was heartbroken for five minutes. Pissed for about a year. Then she started lecturing me about how addiction is a mental illness, and I should be more compassionate."

A low chuckle rumbled in Geo's chest. "Sounds like Ana."

"She's planning to specialize in treating addiction in children."

Geo sat up. "Seriously?"

Will raised himself up and leaned against the headboard. "If you asked her, she'd probably say you helped her find her life's calling. She's not a little girl anymore."

Geo nodded. "I've missed her entire adulthood."

"It doesn't have to stay that way." He reached out and squeezed Geo's hand.

Geo stared at him in amazement. Could it be this simple? Could he really get his life back?

A voice in the back of his head warned him that he wasn't good enough for the Darcys. Will and Ana were both billionaires, thanks to the company stock they had inherited. Geo had car payments and a one-bedroom condo.

They had never seemed to care about the difference in their financial situations. They had never treated him differently. But of course, he *had* been different. He had lived off the Darcys all through college. When he lost their goodwill, he had nothing else.

He might have ended up in the gutter, but he didn't. He checked into a clinic, got himself clean, and joined the army. He turned his life around by *earning* it. He wasn't dependent on anyone anymore. Everything he was, he had made himself.

Which, frankly, was more than Will could say.

Will was smart and responsible. From all Geo could see, he was good at his job. The fact remained that he wouldn't be CEO if he hadn't been born privileged. And Geo refused to feel that he himself was less worthy because of an accident of birth.

No. Whatever was happening between them, Geo would grab it with both hands and ride it for as long as he could. This time, he would not let go.

Chapter 11

Will woke early the next morning. In the faint light of the rising sun, he watched Geo sleep. The sight filled him with a sense of peace.

Rehashing the past the night before had been difficult. Yet, here they were, still together, trying to find a way.

He wasn't reconciled to what Geo had done to Ana. Thinking he intended to sleep with her had hurt like a son of a bitch. Now, though, Will was adapting to a new reality. One where Geo had never intended to be a husband to Ana. He'd just been looking for a payoff.

Will had always known it was about the money, of course. But he'd thought that Geo was marrying her for her trust fund. Not for what amounted to extortion.

The truth was actually the less horrible option. Geo hadn't planned on betraying Will physically, at least. He hadn't planned on making Ana miserable for the rest of her life in a loveless marriage.

But now Will had something new to be mad about. And even though he'd get over it eventually, it was still painful now.

The pain was something he could deal with later, alone. For now, he would make the most of the time he and Geo had together before Will flew home.

He moved closer, and Geo stirred. Will planted a kiss on his lips. They were warm and soft.

Without opening his eyes, Geo reached an arm around Will's waist and drew him close. Soon they were kissing, and their cocks aligned in the most delicious way. Will moved against him. It wasn't long before Will wanted to move inside him.

As Will got out the lube, Geo's legs fell open for easy access. He needed less prep this time, and it wasn't long before Will was fully seated in that slick heat. His gaze locked with Geo's Caribbean blue eyes.

In a slow, sultry rhythm, they made love wordlessly. Their bodies hadn't forgotten how to do this, how to wring out every drop of pleasure from the other. Will could see from Geo's blissful expression and his leaking cock that the angle was perfect to hit his sweet spot. And Will did, over and over again.

Will leaned in for a kiss, and Geo did not disappoint. He parted his lips and their tongues swept together. Each caress built the pleasure between them, until Will knew he couldn't hold back.

"Touch yourself," Will said in Geo's ear, and Geo did. The sight of it amplified Will's desire. His strokes grew harder, deeper, more insistent. And when Geo came, Will followed.

The pleasure rushed over him in endless swells, as if time no longer had meaning. When his breathing finally slowed, he pressed his forehead to Geo's. "Love you."

"Love you, too."

They cleaned up and lazed in bed awhile before showering. Then they enjoyed a long breakfast. Room service had brought omelets this time. Geo put salsa on his, a change from when he lived in Philly. Will tried it, and considered the experiment a success.

"You're not going to work this morning, are you?" Geo asked, his tone a gentle scold.

Will sighed. "I should."

"It's Sunday."

"It's Monday in Hong Kong."

"No," Geo said, "it's ten o'clock Sunday night in Hong Kong. Don't think you can bullshit me."

Will gave him a coy smile. "Look. I appreciate your concern, and I understand the need for work-life balance. My Monday will go better if I work a few hours this morning to plan my week. Then I can go to the vineyard, relax, and have fun."

"Doesn't your assistant keep your calendar?"

"Yes, but I schedule in time to think and make decisions. That's an important part of my job."

Geo eyed him sideways. "I *suppose*."

"You're being a smartass."

"Yes, but you like it."

Will grinned at him. Spending quiet time like this with Geo felt domestic and wonderful. "Will you sleep here tonight?" He was careful to phrase it as a question this time.

"What if someone from Crisanto sees me coming out of the hotel at seven forty-five on a Monday morning?"

Will thought a moment. "Tell them you had a breakfast meeting with Mandie. I'll clear it with her first."

Geo shook his head. He wore a teasing smile. "You used to be so straight-laced. Now you're asking me to lie."

"Fine. Mandie can join us for coffee tomorrow morning."

"Whatever you say, boss."

Will had a few ideas for how to wipe that smirk off his face. But there was no time for that if Will wanted to finish his Sunday routine before they left for the vineyard. Oscar's family had Mass at ten-thirty, and they would all leave in the company van right after.

"I should probably drive home and get clothes for tomorrow," Geo said. "No point sitting around here while you ignore me. Meet you at Crisanto at noon?"

"Sounds like a plan."

But when Geo left, Will didn't get to work right away as he had planned. Instead, he Skyped with Ana. She wasn't on call for a change, and she looked rested and relaxed.

Her wavy blonde hair was tied back in a ponytail. Yoga pants and a white sweatshirt hugged her slender frame. She looked young and innocent, like springtime. For a moment, he just drank in the sight of her. Their schedules were so demanding, they barely saw each other anymore.

When he told her he had run into Geo in Dallas, she was wary. When he said they were taking steps to repair their friendship, she was thrilled.

But when he told her they had dated in college, she was furious that he had kept that fact from her for so long.

"So all this time," she said, "you've been asking me not to contact Geo because you were *jealous* of me."

Will startled at that. "Of course not. I was protecting you. The man got you drunk on your eighteenth birthday and tried to marry you for your trust fund."

"Oh, right, but you're over that now."

"I'm trying."

"So—what. You want my permission to sleep with him? Is that what this is about?"

Will's cheeks heated.

"Ugh, no," she said. "You already slept with him. That's gross. It's a good thing you're a thousand miles away. If you were here, I would kill you."

Will's stomach bottomed out. "You object to us dating, then?"

"I object to you lying about the nature of your relationship with him for...what, thirteen years? Thirteen *years*, Will!"

"Well, yes, that is unfortunate."

She stared at him, her cheeks flushed. "Fortune had nothing to do with it. You withheld information from me. If I'd known the truth, I'd have tried to contact him in Afghanistan. There were nights I woke up in a cold sweat, worrying he was in danger."

He nodded at that, his throat closing. It didn't bear thinking about.

She narrowed her eyes at him, then continued. "But I decided it was more important to make you happy than to reach out to a man who was putting his life in danger, protecting our country. And all because you were afraid your ex-boyfriend might fall for your sister."

"I was not..." But Will couldn't make himself say the words. That was exactly what he had been afraid of. That Geo would come back into Ana's life, and they would fall in love. Because that would have shattered Will. He could not have lived with that.

"I'm sorry," he said to his sister. "I was wrong."

"Hell yeah, you were."

It took him an hour to calm her. In the end, she gave them her blessing. But she was still pissed. He supposed she would be for a long time.

He took a walk outside to clear his head. Memories floated through his mind. He hadn't come out to her until after the Vegas debacle. He couldn't tell her then about his relationship with Geo, because she was still grieving the loss of him. After that, when he wasn't part of their lives anymore, there didn't seem to be a point.

And the fact was, it had hurt too much to think about. It still hurt. No matter where his relationship with Geo went from here, the old pain would always be a part of him.

Apparently, the thought of Geo with a woman made Will insanely jealous. It made him think about Vegas, about how Geo had abandoned him. Just like his parents had abandoned him. Just like Geo's parents had. And now, Ana was mad at him, too.

She would get over it, right? Ana would never break ties with him. They had been close all their lives.

He re-entered the hotel feeling worse than before he left. He could not get the image out of his mind of Ana and Geo at the chapel. About to say their wedding vows. About to drive Will from their lives forever.

The only two people left in the world who loved him unconditionally. He could not afford to lose them.

Chapter 12

Geo had just finished getting his clothes together for Monday when his phone sounded. It was an unknown number with a 215 area code. *Philadelphia.* Butterflies somersaulted in his stomach as he answered. "This is Geo."

"Why, hello, Geo, this is Georgiana Darcy." Her tone was as smooth as butter.

A huge grin split his face. "Ana Banana!" he said automatically, before emotion clogged his throat.

She giggled. "No one has called me that in ten years. How the hell are you?"

He sank onto the bed, relief flooding him. He'd missed her so damn much. Tears burned his eyes. "I'm great. It's good to hear your voice, sweetheart. I understand you're a pediatrician now."

"Finishing up my residency. I understand you're sleeping with my brother now."

He laughed aloud. "You never were one to mince words."

"He never told me you two were a couple. All this time, I thought he was trying to protect me, and he was *jealous* of me."

Geo sat up straighter. "You think?"

"Hell, yes. Which is stupid, because the marriage wouldn't have been legal. I never would have married you sober."

"I'm so sorry, Ana. It was a shitty thing to do, getting you drunk like that—"

"You didn't get me drunk," she said with a laugh. "We had five bottles of Cristal in our suite when you got there. The only reason I invited Tarriqua's sister along was so she could buy us booze. We were hella stupid. That wasn't your fault."

"I should have protected you, and instead, I took advantage of you."

"Yeah, but what a fun story it would have made, if we'd actually gotten married. Can you imagine?"

Geo sat in stunned silence a moment. "Does Will know you're a party girl?"

"I shield him from the worst of it. Besides, that part of my life is mostly over anyway. Med school took care of that. And I'm married now. Did Will tell you? My husband is, like, the steadiest guy I know. Except for Will, of course."

Warmth blossomed in Geo's chest. "I'm glad you're happy, Banana."

"I miss you like crazy. We'll get together soon, okay?"

"Definitely."

"And Geo," she said, her voice tightening, "I used to check your Facebook page every day while you were in Afghanistan. I prayed for you so hard. I can't even tell you how relieved I was when you finally came home. I'm so proud of you."

Emotion swamped him again. He swallowed and said, "Thank you."

"Don't let Will push you around. He can be a prick sometimes, but he's a big softie inside."

"Yeah, I know." It was a moment before he could speak. "Love you, Banana."

"Love you, too."

He ended the call and sat in silence. Just like that, his world had righted itself. Ana had forgiven him—

apparently a long time ago. He felt lighter than he could ever remember feeling.

But was she right—had Will been jealous all this time? That would explain his reaction to Suki. Geo had dealt with jealousy from boyfriends before, and he hadn't put up with it. He wasn't about to put up with it from Will, either.

Geo was the first to arrive at the Crisanto parking lot. Being early was unusual for him. He was eager to see Will again. The morning had been promising.

Will was thinking about their future. The thought made Geo happy. He wanted a future with Will.

As usual, though, Will had taken charge. Rather than asking what Geo wanted, Will had proposed his own scheme. But the idea of living in two cities didn't appeal to Geo. At least not in the long term.

He'd rather find a new job in Philly. He didn't need Will arranging his career.

Being married to his company's CEO would come with challenges. Some people would think he had slept his way to the top—there'd be no getting around that perception. On top of that, his managers would treat him differently. He'd never know whether his success came from his own achievements or from Will.

Despite his submissive streak, Geo wanted to succeed or fail on his own merits. He didn't want Will in charge of his life. Maybe Pemberley wasn't the place for him.

The sound of footsteps interrupted his thoughts. Mandie and Jared approached. Geo took Mandie's left hand. Sure enough, she wore a fancy engagement ring—a big center stone with sprays of tiny diamonds.

"Ha!" Geo said. "If I were a betting man, Will would owe me ten bucks. I told him Jared was going to propose."

She punched his arm. "How did you know?"

"Remember what I said last night about Jared keeping a *good* secret from you?"

She beamed. "That was very clever. I might not fire you after all."

He liked the fact that she was teasing him. It was a good sign. "Thanks for the vote of confidence." He shook Jared's hand. "Congratulations. Take good care of her."

"I will." Jared pulled her close and kissed the top of her head.

"It turns out," she said to Geo, "this ring is the reason he postponed the trip. It's custom, and they were late finishing it."

"I would have come without it," Jared added, "and proposed when she got home. But then my mom came down with a cold when she was supposed to babysit my nieces yesterday morning... I decided waiting an extra day to fly out wouldn't kill us."

Geo spotted Will walking toward them, hands in the pockets of his dark wool coat. Geo's insides turned to mush at the sight of him. They still had things to work out, but Geo trusted they could get through it.

Will congratulated Mandie and Jared when he heard their news. Then, he put his arm around Geo and said to Mandie, "You're having coffee with us tomorrow morning. That way, if anyone sees Geo leaving the hotel on the way to work, Geo can honestly say he had a breakfast meeting with you."

"So...covering up your booty calls is now part of my job description?" she said in a teasing tone. But really, Geo thought she was kind of pissed.

"No. I'm asking you as a friend."

She chuckled and said, "I don't recall hearing a question in there."

Will let out a sigh. "Mandie, will you do me the honor of joining Geo and me for coffee tomorrow morning?"

"I would be delighted." She turned to Jared. "Keep this on the down low. Geo could be fired if his boss finds out he's sleeping with the CEO."

"I thought *you* were his boss," Jared said to her.

"Dotted line."

"What does that even mean?" Jared asked.

"Functionally, he reports to me. Administratively, he reports to the Crisanto CEO through their legal department. And the Crisanto CEO doesn't like employees dating."

Jared scowled. "That's pretty old-school."

"It is," Will agreed. "And eventually, we'll change the policy. For now, we're choosing our battles."

Will slid his arm down Geo's back and pulled away. It was the circumspect thing to do. Still, Geo missed the warmth of him.

A little part of him, though, was doing a Snoopy dance. Three people in the world now knew he and Will were dating. Which was three more than when they had dated in college. That was progress.

Chanisse arrived with the keys to the company van, and they piled inside. When the rest of the group followed a few minutes later, they headed out of the city and into the countryside.

Geo fidgeted during the trip. He wanted to touch Will. Tried to figure out ways to brush against him. His skin heated with the thought of it, of being flesh-against-flesh with the man.

He also wanted to tell Will about the phone call from Ana. But that, too, would have to wait until they could be alone.

The vineyard was a gently sloping tract that stretched for acres under a wide blue sky. The winery sat nestled among low trees. It was a huge wood-frame building with a tasting room and gift shop.

A pond separated it from the family home and the guest house. Trails led through the garden. Most of the plants were dormant, but a few evergreens and berry-laden hollies added color.

Oscar introduced his brother, who took them on a short tour of the vineyard. Admittedly, it wasn't much to see, mostly wooden posts and leafless vines. But it was good to take a long walk out of the city and breathe the fresh, cool air.

Oscar's children played with their cousins, running around among the rows. The sound of their laughter brought a wistful feeling to Geo's heart.

When he and Will had dated in college, they had discussed having kids. They were thirty-two now. It was time.

But was Will ready for that? Was Geo getting ahead of himself? They had so much to figure out, and Will was boarding a plane on Friday. Once he left, it would be easy to forget what they had shared here. Geo couldn't let that happen.

When the others entered the tasting room, Geo hung back. Will stayed with him. They stood near the pond, ducks swimming among the reeds.

"Go inside," Geo said. "Have fun. I'll be fine."

"I'd rather stay with you."

Geo raised his brows. "Aren't you afraid of offending Oscar?"

"He'll understand."

Geo wasn't sure he would, but let the subject drop. Will had made up his mind. He wouldn't change it without a detailed and persuasive argument that would probably take longer than the actual wine tasting.

Which, Geo supposed, was one of the things that made Will a good CEO. Often making *any* decision was better than making no decision. It gave you a path forward, and you could course correct as new information came to light. Constantly second guessing yourself would only drive you and the people around you crazy.

So Geo took the opportunity to talk to him about Ana. "Your sister called me this morning."

Will's lips tightened. "I expected she would, after I gave her your number. You two clear the air?"

"We did." He narrowed his brow in contemplation. "I think she gave us her blessing."

The corner of Will's mouth quirked upward, but then fell again. "She's pissed at me for not telling her about us sooner."

"I got that impression." Geo grinned. "It's fine, though, right? You two will work through it."

Will shrugged. "Eventually. She made me realize what an asshole I was to you. I should have come out the first time you asked me to. My father would have been fine with it." He shook his head. "I don't know what I was afraid of."

"It was a different time. Don't Ask, Don't Tell was a thing. Same-sex marriage was legal in only a handful of states. You weren't ready." Geo's chest tightened. "I shouldn't have pressured you."

"I made you feel like a second-class citizen."

Geo nodded. "I wouldn't have thrown away what we had over it, if I'd known how rare it was. That's the problem with finding your soulmate at eighteen. You think love is easy. You don't realize until you lose it how hard love really is."

Will shoved his hands into his pockets. "I wish I could touch you."

He eyed Will for a long time. "Maybe we should come clean with Oscar. I'd have to resign, but the fact is, my position is going to be eliminated anyway."

Will looked off toward the horizon.

"It's fine," Geo continued. "I'll move to Philly and find a job there. I have some savings to tide me over."

"Let's not rush into anything," Will said. "It will be at least a month before we eliminate any positions, maybe longer. I prefer attrition and early retirement where possible."

"And what about us?" Geo asked. "I don't want a long-distance relationship. And I don't want to fly back and forth between Dallas and Philly. Not for more than a few months. All that time on a plane would drive me crazy. I'm not like you. I can't sit quietly for long periods of time—I need action."

"It doesn't make sense for you to quit your job and leave Dallas until we know where this relationship is headed."

Geo felt the words like a stab to the gut. "I already know what I want."

Will looked at him searchingly. "So do I. But relationships take time to develop."

Anger surged in Geo's chest. "Is this just a fling to you?"

"Of course not. I want this to work out." Will spoke intensely. Then, his tone softened. "You said yourself, it's too soon to uproot your life. There are no guarantees."

"So what you're saying is, you haven't really forgiven me."

Will bristled. "Not at all. I'm thinking about *your* needs. I can't ask you to do something irrevocable. Not yet."

Geo kicked the dirt with the toe of his shoe. "I was crazy to think I could ever be good enough for you."

"What?" Will's voice was sharp. "When have I given you reason to think—"

"It's in everything you say and do. Always has been." Geo met his eyes. "You make decisions and expect me to go along."

Will shook his head. "I do that with everyone. I did it with Mandie this morning, and she called me on it. You can do that, too. I don't want to impose my wishes on you. Just speak up."

"Or maybe you could try to be more considerate?"

Will's voice rose. "I *do* try. I'm not perfect, Geo. I make mistakes all the time." He paced, the dry grass crunching under his feet. "If you need something from me, just ask. I'm not a mind reader."

Geo walked toward the pond. Sunlight shimmered on the surface, but the depths were murky. He couldn't believe this was happening. He was ready to change his whole life for Will, and the guy was acting like it was an imposition.

He tried skipping stones across the water, but he'd never been any good at that. Will walked up beside him. "This is going to take time, Geo. As much as we both want it, we can't change our lives in the course of a weekend."

"We can," Geo pleaded. "We can make this work if we both commit to it." His throat tightened as Will's expression remained impassive. "But you're not willing to do that."

Will's voice grew rough with emotion. "I've been dead inside since the day we broke up. Now I feel alive again. I'm a hundred percent committed."

Geo's heart swelled and his mind raced. He didn't want to wait a moment longer than necessary to start their future together. "Then let's tell Oscar. I'll give my notice and move to Philadelphia once my two weeks are up."

Will pulled back, his face turning pensive. He looked out over the water. "I'd prefer to avoid telling Oscar about us right now. We're still in some sensitive negotiations, and I don't want to alienate him."

Geo scoffed. Typical Will, choosing caution over taking a chance. Geo eyed the weeping willows that edged the pond, their branches gray and bare in the cold winter air. "Of course. Business first."

"Not always. But in this case, yes."

Frustration built up inside Geo. "You can be a real prick sometimes."

Will glowered. "I don't deny that. I'm doing what I think is best. I'm sorry you disagree."

"It's always going to be like this with you." Geo couldn't stop the anger from lacing his tone.

"Like what?"

"I'll never be your first consideration."

Will turned silent. Finally, he said, "I understand why you feel that way. You're first in my heart."

"I'm not. If you had to choose between me and Ana, you'd choose Ana."

It was a low blow, dredging up the past like that. But Geo wasn't about to let Will pretend that Geo was his top priority when he wasn't.

Will said in a clipped tone, "Do you expect to put me in a position again where I'll have to make that choice?"

Geo shook his head. His lungs deflated. "Of course not."

"Then how does it even signify? She was eighteen, Geo. Barely more than a child. Of course I chose her. She needed me."

"I needed you," Geo growled.

"On the contrary. As soon as I walked away, you managed to get sober. Apparently I was holding you back."

Geo's eyes widened, and his jaw grew slack. "That isn't true. *I* was holding me back. I let myself become dependent. I thought I couldn't live without you. It was only when I had no other choice that I discovered how strong I was."

Will looked at him intently, his expression softening. In a low voice, he asked, "Why are we fighting?"

Geo swallowed the knot in his throat. "I don't know. I guess we've got a lot of baggage to work through. But the only way to do that is together. I don't want to be in Dallas while you're in Philly."

"I don't want that, either." Will's jaw clenched. The ducks splashed in the water as they dunked their heads.

"Can we find a solution that doesn't involve telling Oscar about us?"

Geo sighed. He considered a moment. "How about this. Tomorrow I'll give my notice. I'll wrap things up here and move to Philly as soon as I can. Becca will give me a nice reference."

"How about you wait a week to give your notice? I don't want anything to disrupt our negotiations."

Geo rolled his eyes. "Fine."

"You don't sound happy."

No, because once again, Will was calling the shots. But Geo didn't bother pointing that out. The guy seemed incapable of seeing it.

Instead, Geo said, "I'm upending my entire life. Of course I'm not happy."

Will took a step closer, maybe too close. "But we'll be together," he said in a low voice, so kind and hopeful that Geo's heart turned to liquid.

"If things work out for us," Geo said, his chest tight, "it will be worth it. If they don't…" He swallowed the lump in his throat. "At least we can say we tried."

Will looked away. The emotion between them was far too intense for this setting. Oscar's kids and their cousins were chasing each other through the garden trails, his wife watching them. Will and Geo had to be careful not to give too much away.

"I'm sorry things are so complicated," Will said. "Can I do something to make it easier for you?"

"Life is always complicated. I appreciate the offer, but I need to do this on my own."

"If you insist."

Geo met his eyes. "I do."

Chanisse came out and joined them. She looked cold in a gray trench coat, black gloves on her hands.

"Mandie and Suki seem to be on a shopping spree," she said as she approached. "I had to get out of there before I maxed out my credit card. At my age, I should be getting rid of things, not buying new."

Geo nodded. "How's the wine?"

She tilted her head. "I like my reds a little drier than what they offer," she said in her soft contralto. "They've got some nice dessert wine blends, though. Will, you should try some. Maybe have a bottle or two shipped home. I can keep Geo company."

Will nodded. At her urging, he seemed to accept that Oscar would be offended if Will didn't at least taste his brother's wine. So Will sauntered off, leaving Geo alone with Chanisse.

Looking off into the distance, she said to Geo, "Well, this is a fine mess you've gotten yourself into."

His senses went on high alert. "What do you mean?"

"You're falling in love with that man. And don't tell me you're not, because I've been around the block a few times."

Geo's cheeks heated. "Is it that obvious? Do you think Oscar suspects?"

"Oscar? No. Suki? Definitely. Would you like a little unsolicited advice?"

"From you? Always."

"Someone with your education and skills will always be able to find a job. But love? That's a rare thing. I hope you're not dazzled, though, by Will's money and power. Men like that can easily find companionship. Whether they want commitment is another question."

Geo hadn't thought about it in those terms before. Will had been born wealthy and privileged. But he hadn't been one to lord it over other people. No, he just had an unconscious expectation that everyone would cater to him.

Could Geo live with that? "He's worth taking a chance on."

Chanisse nodded thoughtfully. "In that case, I wish you all the best. But don't give your heart too fast. And don't let him take advantage of you. Hold on to your self-respect. Don't do anything to compromise it."

Was Geo doing that? Was he giving Will the upper hand in order to get what he wanted in return? Because the truth was, if they started out that way, Geo would have a hard time getting his power back.

"That's good advice," he said. "I appreciate it."

She shook her head. "I don't know what Oscar was thinking, bringing us out here in the winter, and you unable to drink."

He smiled. "He's proud of his brother."

"For good reason. This place is impressive. But it wasn't very kind to you."

"I don't expect people to consider my addiction when making plans."

"But they should," she insisted. "With Oscar's commitment to mental health, he should have been more mindful."

She eyed him, wearing a thoughtful expression. "I know Becca's been mentoring you. With her out of town... You can come to me if you need to talk about anything—personal or professional. I can't imagine what it must be like for you, without parents or siblings to rely on."

He nodded pensively. "Thanks, Chanisse. I may take you up on that."

Suki came out of the gift shop laden with shopping bags. Geo excused himself to Chanisse and walked over in Suki's direction. She handed him two bags of wine to carry for her, and they walked together to the van.

"So you liked the wine?" he asked as they headed across the gravel.

She chuckled. "I don't have a sophisticated palate, like Chanisse does."

He raised his brows in surprise. "Did she say that to you?"

"No, she'd never say something like that. She was thinking it, though. Not that she's wrong." Suki eyed him sideways. "So what's the deal with you and Will?"

Geo gave her a flirty smile. "He's just keeping me company."

"He's been keeping you company a lot lately."

With that, Geo reached his limit. He didn't like her tone of voice, or the implied threat. Oscar had her ear, and everyone knew it.

As they loaded the bags into the van, Geo replied, "Suki, I don't know what you want me to say. When I first started working for Crisanto, I wanted to ask you out. I even went as far as talking to Becca about updating the fraternization policy. Oscar wouldn't hear of it. So if I happen to enjoy Will's company, that's not a reflection on you. I enjoy your company, too, but I can't date you. End of story."

She set her hands on her hips. "So you're not dating Will?"

"He's going back to Philadelphia at the end of this week. The only way I could date him would be to leave Crisanto."

She nodded at that. Geo didn't feel bad about deceiving her. She was poking her nose into his personal business. Besides, what he had said was true, if misleading.

Mandie and Jared exited the shop and joined them by the van. "Well, that put a nice dent in my Christmas shopping list," she said.

"And Hanukkah shopping," Jared added.

"Having it all shipped?" Geo asked.

"No room in my luggage," Mandie said. "I think Oscar twisted Will's arm into buying a case for his sister."

Geo chuckled. "Poor Ana. She's more of a Cristal girl."

Mandie drew her brow. "Will told you that?"

Shit. Geo would have to be more careful. "How else would I know?"

Chanisse came over. "Those poor ducks look cold, swimming on that water."

"It *is* pretty here," Mandie said, looking around. "Must be spectacular in the spring."

"I hope you have a chance to come see it again," Suki said to her.

"Me too." Mandie squeezed her hand.

Will and Oscar joined them. The kids waved goodbye to their cousins, and they all got into the van for the ride home. Jared kept checking his phone for the time. They were dropping him off at the airport on the way.

At the curb in front of the terminal, Mandie said goodbye to him with an unabashed kiss. Then, she and Suki talked nonstop on the way back. Geo suspected Mandie was distracting herself.

How hard would it be when Will flew out on Friday? Would he ever see the man again? They could make plans now, but it would be at least a month before Geo could relocate to Philly. A lot could change in a month.

The thought made his chest ache.

Once they reached downtown, Will and Mandie entered the hotel through the front door. Geo took a detour through the parking garage. Not only would it help deflect Suki's suspicions, it also gave him the chance to pick up his suit from the car.

Back in Will's suite, Will followed him into the bedroom as he hung up the suit. Then, they fell into a long embrace. Geo's body tingled at the touch as he breathed in Will's scent of sandalwood and clean musk.

"I hated not being able to touch you all day," Will said, greedy hands running down the length of Geo's back.

"Me, too." He gave the man a toe-curling kiss.

Will met his gaze, deep sadness in his eyes. "Could we be kidding ourselves? Could the sex be blinding us to the challenges of a real relationship?"

Geo wanted to rail at the suggestion, but it was a fair question. In bed, everything between them was magical. The rest of the time, they seemed to struggle.

"When we dated in college," Geo said, "things weren't always easy, were they?"

"We argued sometimes," Will conceded. A grin lit his features. "But making up was worth it."

"Did you ever doubt that we belonged together?"

"Not for a moment. Not even when we broke up. I thought that was just...needing some space from each other for a while." Will shook his head. "If I'd known eleven years would go by, I'd have worked harder."

"Me, too." Geo squeezed his hand. "We made so many mistakes then. Let's not repeat them. We need to believe in us, Will. Believe that we were meant to be together."

They ordered room service for dinner because it was easier than going out and worrying about being seen.

Then, they talked for a while about everything and nothing. Will seemed to relax. But later, after they made love, Will grew distant again. Geo didn't know how to reach him. It was like he was floating away, and Geo was powerless to stop it.

Chapter 13

"So what are we supposed to be talking about?" Mandie asked on Monday over breakfast. They were at the dining table in Will's suite, because the stress of not being able to touch Geo in public was making Will cranky. A carafe of coffee sat before them, along with a basket of pastries.

Will was failing at everything. As a boyfriend, as a brother, as a CEO... He hated keeping up this deception about his relationship with Geo. It didn't align with his values. But it was too late to undo it.

"Let's talk about the fraternization policy," Geo said, his brow drawn and lips tight. "It's one big clusterfuck. Suki is jealous of my relationship with Will, even though she and I never dated. And the policy hasn't stopped Will and me from seeing each other. It's just led to us lying about it."

Will tapped his folded copy of *USA Today* on the tabletop. "Not lying, exactly."

Geo's eyes narrowed. "Engaging in deceitful behavior," he rectified. "So overall, the policy is a failure. Oscar won't change it unless Pemberley pressures him to."

"Now is not the time," Will said. "We have bigger concerns, and I don't want to lose his goodwill."

"Fuck you, Mr. CEO," Geo retorted. "You've made up your mind, and you won't even listen to me."

Will's cheeks heated at the outburst. He wasn't surprised that Geo had snapped like that, given the stress he was under. But it was irresponsible to behave that way in front of Mandie.

"Geo," Mandie said sharply, "you may be in Will's hotel suite, but this is a business meeting."

Geo was shaking with rage now. Will set aside the newspaper and apologized to Mandie. Then he took Geo by the hand and led him into the bedroom.

"This is intolerable," Geo said. "Who knows how many other employees are in this situation? I'm quitting in three weeks, and the secrecy is making me insane."

Will cupped Geo's face in his hands. When Geo didn't pull away, Will leaned in and kissed him.

"I understand your frustration," Will said. "This situation has tapped into your anger about the way I treated you in college. I'm sorry I hurt you that way. After this week, it will never happen again."

Geo's eyes glistened. "I feel like your dirty little secret."

Will pressed his forehead to Geo's. "Dirty, yes. But little..." His hand found Geo's groin. "Definitely not."

Geo smiled and gave him a desperate little moan. "Don't start something you can't finish."

Will kissed him deeply. "Maybe we could have a private lunch date."

"It would look suspicious."

"Then I guess we'll have to wait until tonight. You *are* staying here?"

Geo glided his hands up Will's torso and stroked his shoulders. "Absolutely."

They kissed again. Geo seemed calmer. They rejoined Mandie at the dining table in the sitting room.

"Sorry," Geo said to her. "That was unprofessional. It won't happen again."

She nodded. "It's another good example of what a shitty policy it is. It puts people into an intensified emotional state in a workplace environment. But Will's right. We have higher priority concerns, and this is close to Oscar's heart. We need to approach the change carefully."

Geo sank into a chair, looking defeated. "I don't know why I even brought it up."

"Because it matters to you," Will said, standing behind Geo and massaging his shoulders. He loved the feel of those strong muscles underneath his hands. "It matters to me, too. But we need to compromise on it, for now."

"Maybe we could suggest an employee survey," Mandie said. "Just to get an idea of what people think. Encourage some kind of dialogue with HR, including anonymous feedback."

Will looked at Mandie intently. "Does this create a liability situation for us?"

"Yes," Geo answered sharply.

Mandie nodded. "I agree."

"Okay, Geo," Will said as he sat, "put together a legal argument for why the policy needs to change. Send it to Mandie by the end of the day. We'll decide where to go from there."

"Yes, sir," Geo said, grinning and looking proud. Will loved that look on him.

It was a relief to be on the same side as Geo for once. Things between them seemed precarious right now. It was taking time for them to get on the same wavelength. The thought made Will nervous.

Was that a normal part of adjusting to being a couple? Or was something deeper going on?

Will couldn't bear the thought of losing Geo. It had almost destroyed him the first time. He wouldn't survive if it happened again.

The engineering presentation was running way too long. Will fought the urge to look at the clock, because it was rude and dismissive to do so. But clearly, Henry from engineering was under the mistaken impression that Pemberley wanted to gut the department, and his job was to make sure they didn't.

Henry was going into way too much detail, defending every little project. It was unnecessary. Will wanted to know about the big picture. It was someone else's job to worry about the details.

Finally, the torture came to an end. "Thank you, Henry," Will said. "I'm very impressed by your operation here. Email me the presentation, and I'll forward it to our head of engineering. She'll contact you with any questions."

Will declined Oscar's lunch invitation, wanting to recharge and mentally prepare for the afternoon meetings. They had a full day planned, and he needed to clear his head. Mandie, meanwhile, commandeered an empty office to make some phone calls. So Will was alone in the conference room that had been serving as their make-shift office when Geo dropped in.

With a smile, Geo closed the door behind him. "How was your morning?"

"Is the engineering VP always so boring?"

Geo chuckled. "Pretty much. But his technical knowledge is unsurpassed. And he's a good manager."

Will nodded pensively. "We have a rule at Pemberley. No death by PowerPoint. There's a right way to use that software, and a wrong way."

Geo's brows rose. "I could give a lunch-and-learn on presentation skills—" He broke off, his expression falling. "Except I'm quitting in three weeks."

"I'm sorry." Will rose and placed his hands at Geo's waist. "We can explore other options, look for another position for you at Pemberley."

Geo pulled away. "I told you, I don't need your help."

Will shook his head, then met his lover's eyes. "I'm not talking about special treatment. I'm here to smooth the transition. To help figure out what to do about displaced employees. It's just a matter of adding your name to a list that HR will work with."

"What if we get married?" Geo asked. "What will it be like for me, if everyone sees me as the CEO's husband? I'll lose my identity. I don't want that."

Will thought about that a moment. "Fair enough. Perhaps we should wait to cross that bridge when we come to it."

Geo walked to the window and looked out over the city. Will walked up behind him.

"What it comes down to," Geo said, "is that you're not as committed to this relationship as I am."

Will took his hand. "That isn't fair."

"Isn't it? Because I feel like I've been the one pursuing *you* from the beginning. You could have almost any man you want, Mr. Billionaire CEO. Why would you settle for a nobody like me?"

Will gazed at him, wondering where Geo's insecurities were coming from. Will said fervently, "I'm thirty-two years old, and you're the only man I've ever loved. I want to settle down and start a family. And you're the one I want to do that with. You've always been the one. And now that I've got you back, I won't let anything come between us."

Geo smiled softly, his eyes misting. "That's all I needed to hear." He pulled Will in for a kiss.

Will stepped back. "Is the door locked?"

"Don't know." Geo kissed him again.

"We can't do this if the door is unlocked."

"Live a little." Geo pulled him close and plundered his mouth.

And just that quickly, Will was lost. Lost in the love and desire and promise this man offered. For ten years, Will couldn't picture his future. Now he could see everything.

Geo in his kitchen, helping the housekeeper make peach cobbler just the way Will liked it. A little girl and a little boy, a couple of years apart, running around and getting into mischief. And as the years went by, they would graduate from college, leaving him and Geo as empty nesters, grayer but just as happy, content in the life they had built together.

The sound of the door opening broke his reverie. He jumped back. For a millisecond, he hoped it was Mandie. But then he looked up to see Oscar's dark and angry eyes.

Shit, shit, shit.

Oscar closed the door behind him. "What is this?"

"I—I'm sorry, Oscar," Will stammered. "This... I... We shouldn't have gone behind your back. I take full responsibility."

"You seduced my legal counsel?" Oscar raged. "The one who's supposed to protect me from you?"

"Forgive me, Oscar," Geo said in a calming tone. "I know I let you down, and I'm sorry about that. But let's be clear. Will didn't seduce me. If anything, it was the other way around. It has nothing to do with my duties to Crisanto."

"How can it not?"

"With all due respect," Geo said, "I'm not your legal counsel, Oscar. I work for Crisanto—which is now a wholly owned subsidiary of Pemberley Industries. It's not my job to represent you or Crisanto against Will or Pemberley. It's my job to look out for the combined interests of the two entities."

"We have a strict fraternization policy here. You know that."

"I do," Geo agreed. "I realize this is a technicality, but it covers Crisanto employees dating each other. It doesn't cover a Crisanto employee dating a Pemberley employee. The policy needs to be updated to reflect the new corporate structure."

"It's just words, Geo," Oscar raged. "You know my feelings about this sort of behavior. You flaunted them because you thought you could get away with it if you dated the new CEO. Well, that doesn't fly with me. I'm still your boss, and you betrayed my trust."

"I'm sorry—"

"It's too late for apologies. You're fired. Security will escort you to clean out your desk and leave the building."

Geo paled and looked chagrined. Will wanted to take his hand but didn't dare.

"As for you," Oscar said, turning to Will, "I thought I could trust you. I sold my business to you because I thought we shared the same values. Clearly I was wrong about that. The rest of our meetings today are canceled. I'm calling Becca to see what can be done about this debacle."

With that, he left the room, slamming the door behind him. Will stood frozen, stunned. How had this happened?

"I'm sorry, Will," Geo said in low tones.

Anger rose up from Will's gut. "You couldn't just do as I asked," he said as he packed up his computer. "I told you no kissing unless the door was locked."

"Will, that's not—"

"You've always been impulsive and irresponsible. But then, you were planning to quit anyway. Meanwhile, I've spent a year working on this merger. Without Oscar's cooperation, it could all go to hell. Because you couldn't keep your hands to yourself."

Geo didn't respond, just looked at him icily. Will stormed out, unsure where he was going. He headed back to the hotel because he didn't know what else to do.

He needed to work off some of his anger. He dropped off his computer in his room, changed out of his suit, and went outside for a walk.

The air was cool, the sun bright. Will marched forward, hands in his pockets, eyes unseeing. When had he turned into such a fuck-up?

Oscar's anger had been predictable. Will should have prepared a response just in case. After all, he and Geo had been skirting the edge for days. Instead of handling the situation like the CEO he was, he'd stammered like an idiot. Geo had been the one to take control of the situation.

His heart ached at the memory of Geo's cold expression as Will had left. His gut tightened. He had made a bad situation worse with his reaction.

He looked up to discover he was approaching the Kennedy Memorial near Dealey Plaza. Maybe some unconscious part of his mind knew he needed to be there. Knew he needed a reminder of how life could change in an instant. How great promise could be lost.

How something you took for granted could disappear from your life, and nothing would ever be the same again.

Why had Will said those things? He hadn't been speaking to the Geo of today. He'd been speaking to the Geo of ten years ago, treating the situation as black and white—and blaming Geo for his own mistakes.

When they were kissing in the conference room, Will could have pulled away and locked the damn door. He was the one who had something at stake, not Geo. It was Will's responsibility to act. But Geo had been a convenient scapegoat.

Dread rushed over him. Will walked briskly back to the hotel. Geo wasn't there, and his gym bag was gone. He didn't pick up when Will called his cell.

I'm an ass, Will texted. *I'm sorry. Where are you?*

He waited for a response. An hour went by. Then another. Despite three more texts, Geo didn't respond.

As night fell, Will sat on the floor in the dark, cell phone in hand. Fate had given him a second chance, and he had blown it.

This time, it was all on him.

Two days passed. Geo didn't answer his phone or return texts. No one at Crisanto could get hold of him. Panicked, Ian from HR gave Geo's home address to Will, so he and Mandie could check up on him.

Geo didn't answer his door, either. Will called 911.

A neighbor came to see what the trouble was. He had a spare key, he said. But he'd seen Geo leave in a taxi two days earlier, suitcase in hand. Still, he gave the key to the police, and they went inside. The house was empty.

As Mandie drove the company van back to Crisanto, she said, "He needs time, Will. He just lost his job—"

"This isn't about his job. It's about me. He was planning to quit and move to Philly so we could be together. But I fucked that up. I said awful things to him. I regretted them almost as soon as I said them. But by then, it was too late."

"Wait," Mandie said. "Back up. He was planning to give up his job and his home for you, when he'd known you a week?"

Will let out a deep sigh. "Geo and I...dated in college."

Mandie let out a strangled cry of frustration. "And you're just telling me this *now*?"

Will didn't know what to say to that. He was too numb to care about Mandie's opinion at the moment. "Admittedly, I haven't shown the best judgment in this whole affair."

"Ya think?"

He clenched his jaw. It took a moment for his mind to clear. "In all fairness, I hadn't seen him in a decade. I walked into that room expecting Becca to be there, not the man I'd been pining over for ten years."

"So Geo was negotiating on behalf of Crisanto, when the other party was a man he'd secretly been intimate with."

"No. I mean, yes, but there were no negotiations. Geo clarified a couple of points in the contract. You said yourself it was nothing."

"Nothing except a potential conflict of interest. Will, you need to disclose this to Oscar. I realize he's still pissed at you, but if this goes on any longer... I mean, if you don't tell him, I'll have to."

Will closed his eyes. "Fuck."

"I knew it was a mistake to write up that contract saying you and Geo could sleep together."

He let out a frustrated laugh. "Don't beat yourself up. We'd have slept together either way. I was so far gone. Damn it, I'm in love with him."

Mandie nodded. "Okay, so. Oscar values family above everything, right? Play that up. Geo is the love of your life, the one who got away. When you first saw him in that conference room, you were so surprised, you lost your head. You made a terrible mistake, hiding the truth, and you regret it. You're coming clean now because you value your business relationship with him and you respect him as a man. You promise that nothing like this will happen again. Agreed?"

"Agreed. And then I'm going to find Geo."

"How?"

"I know people at Homeland Security," he said drily.

"Will," she scolded.

"Fine, I won't break the law. Geo must have someone he confides in. He's a sociable person. Someone at Crisanto must know where he went."

"I have an idea," Mandie said. "In fact, it might be the answer to both problems."

The following morning, Will sat with Mandie in the Crisanto conference room. His foot tapped the floor. He hoped this wouldn't take long. He had a plane to catch.

Oscar entered looking pissed. After three days, Will was tired of that expression. As Becca had said when Will called her, it was an emotional issue for both him and Oscar. And neither was on good terms with his emotions.

Oscar closed the door and pulled out a chair. "Becca said I should listen to what you have to say," he snarled as he sat.

"I owe you an apology," Will began, speaking the words he'd memorized ahead of time. "I've not been completely honest with you. The fact is, Geo and I dated in college. Last Monday, when I saw him again, I couldn't think clearly. This was a man I once wanted to marry. I was in shock."

Oscar gazed at Will in stunned silence, his eyes wide. Then, he turned to Mandie. "Did you know about this?"

"Not until yesterday."

Will continued, "Things ended badly between Geo and me. We were young and stupid... We hadn't seen each other in ten years. It's no excuse, but I hope it's an explanation for our unprofessional behavior."

Oscar didn't quite meet Will's eyes, just nodded. At least he didn't look pissed anymore.

"I'm sorry for the difficult position we put you in," Will said. "Geo wanted to tell you the truth. I was concerned it might distract from the negotiations. Or maybe I was just embarrassed. I didn't know what to say to you. I've never let my personal life affect my professional relationships this way. I apologize for the distress I caused you."

"Oscar," Mandie said, "for the sake of Crisanto, I hope you can accept Will's apology. This was an extraordinary situation. It's not something that will be repeated."

Oscar turned to Will. "You mean you don't have boy toys scattered about the country for your convenience?"

"That's uncalled for," Mandie said.

"You're right," Oscar said, his smirk fading. He made eye contact with Will. "I'm sorry."

"Please understand," Will said. "Geo is the love of my life. I want to raise a family with him. We should have been more circumspect in an office environment. But I make no apologies for entering into a romantic relationship with him during this trip."

Oscar cleared his throat. "Yes. Of course. The Pemberley policy is more liberal than the one we have at Crisanto. Our fraternization policy—"

"Is not defensible in court," Mandie said. "As Becca has been telling you for years. By firing Geo the way you did, you opened Crisanto—and Pemberley—to a lawsuit we would lose. I've drawn up a severance agreement to hopefully prevent such action. I'll present it to Geo as soon as we figure out how to get hold of him."

Oscar stared at her a long time. "He broke the rules."

"Rules that should never have been in place," Mandie said. "They virtually ensure that employees will go behind their boss's back if they want to date. The Pemberley policy requires transparency. The relationship must be disclosed, and protections set into place to prevent favoritism, and to prevent retaliation if things go wrong."

"Oscar," Will said, "under the new corporate structure, you don't need to concern yourself with these policy issues anymore. Let's leave these discussions to the lawyers."

Oscar opened his mouth to speak, but Will continued. "You and I are businesspeople, and I hope we're also friends. I realize I've damaged your trust. Tell me what you need from me to repair this relationship."

Oscar crossed his arms and furrowed his brows. "This thing between you and Geo—it's for real? You're planning to marry him?"

Will's face heated. He didn't know how to answer that question. He didn't even know where Geo was.

"We'll need to get reacquainted first," Will said, "before we make any definitive decisions. But I hope we're headed in that direction."

Oscar wagged his head. Then, he rose with a smile. "I guess I can forget about your lie of omission if you forget about the fact that I fired your boyfriend." He held out his hand.

Will stood and shook it gratefully. He was glad that fiasco was behind him. Now to what really mattered— finding Geo and winning his heart. For good, this time.

Chapter 14

"Can I get you anything else, Mrs. O'Leary?" Geo asked Becca's mom. She was a slender woman, her shoulder-length gray hair pulled into a ponytail. "Some tea? A blanket?"

She scowled at him and said in a thin voice, "This is Florida, young man. It's eighty degrees."

He chuckled. "Some iced tea, then? Lemonade?"

"Lemonade would be very nice."

Will went into the kitchen and got the pitcher out of the fridge. Becca said to him, "You know she's conning you. She's perfectly capable of walking on her own. The doctor said the exercise is good for her."

"I don't mind." Geo added some ice to a clear plastic glass and filled it with fresh-squeezed lemonade. Pulp floated on the top. The scent of citrus and sugar made his mouth water.

"I appreciate your being here." Becca's brown eyes gazed at him softly. "It's taken a load off my mind. I've got appointments at two facilities this afternoon. I can rest easy with you keeping an eye on Mom."

"It's my pleasure."

She chuckled. "Looking after a cantankerous old woman?"

"She's not cantankerous. She's sweet. You're blessed to have her."

Becca nodded. "You're right. It's easy to get caught up in the everyday stress and lose sight of the bigger picture. Thank you for reminding me."

He had told her he'd lost his parents as a teenager. In fact, they'd talked about a lot of things. Before he and Will were reunited, he'd mentioned their relationship in college. He hadn't mentioned Will's last name, though.

Should he talk to her about the situation? He worried it might bias her against Will.

Besides, he wasn't sure whether he and Will had any chance for a future. Will clearly didn't trust Geo, and Geo wouldn't tolerate his belittling comments.

Geo forced himself to get out of his head and focus on the present moment. He was here to help Becca.

After a light lunch of Niçoise salad, she left for her appointments. Mrs. O'Leary napped in the sun room, while Geo sat on the deck just outside reading the news on his phone.

The condo sat on the bay. It offered a beautiful view of calm water. Birds like pelicans, egrets, and cormorants fished there. It was no wonder Mrs. O'Leary didn't want to move back to Dallas.

The doorbell rang, and Geo scowled. He didn't think Becca was expecting company. Maybe it was a package or something.

He rose to answer the door, hoping the noise wouldn't disturb Mrs. O'Leary. He looked out the sidelights and froze.

How had Will found him?

The unexpected sight swamped him with emotion. He'd come to Florida because he needed time away to work through all the changes of the past ten days. His life had been turned upside-down, and he didn't know what to think about any of it.

But he couldn't exactly pretend Will wasn't there. The man had seen him. And if Geo didn't let him in, he might start pounding on the door.

So Geo took a deep breath and opened it. His heart thumped, and his head grew light. The shock on Will's face must match his own.

Geo wanted to fall into those strong arms, to feel Will's comfort. But he resisted. If he gave in now, Will would always have the upper hand. Geo would rather end things between them than spend the rest of his life feeling like a second-class citizen, the way he had in college.

"You're here," Will said, his voice barely audible. His Adam's apple bobbed. "Thank God. No one could get hold of you. People at the office have been worried."

"Sorry. I haven't wanted to talk."

"I'm the one who's sorry. I didn't mean the things I said—"

"You did, or you wouldn't have said them," Geo insisted. "You think I'm still the man I was at twenty-two. I served in Afghanistan for six years. I know we haven't talked much about that, but I deserve your respect."

"I know you do. I was wrong, Geo, and I'm sorry. I don't know what else I can say." Will's eyes wore a pleading expression. "Can I come in, so we can talk?"

It took everything Geo had to resist. "I don't think that's a good idea. Becca's mom is sleeping."

Will's eyebrows rose. "Is Becca here?"

"She's touring a couple of assisted living facilities."

Will shook his head. "She was expecting me. Apparently she set this up."

Geo wasn't sure what he thought about that. He wasn't ready to deal with Will right now. "How long will you be in town?"

"As long as it takes to win you back." He looked around, then eyed Geo, a frown on his face. Then, he got down on both knees.

"I'm begging you, Geo. And I will beg every day of my life if I have to. Please forgive me. I was an ass. I love you, and I can't lose you again. My life will never be complete without you."

Geo knew the words were sincere. And he wasn't even angry anymore. But somehow, it wasn't enough.

"You humiliated me."

"I know."

"Do you?" Geo couldn't keep the resentment out of his tone. "I spent twenty-two years feeling like I'd never measure up to you. I can't spend the rest of my life feeling that way. You don't respect me."

Will rose. "I'll fix this."

"I'm not sure it's fixable."

"I'll find a way." He hugged himself. "If you decide you want to see me, I'm staying at the Ritz."

Geo chuckled, but the sound held no mirth. "Of course you are. I'm staying at the Hampton Inn. You should try it sometime. Free parking, free breakfast, free Wi-Fi. It's awesome."

Will paled. Maybe he was finally getting it, the gulf between them. And how far he'd have to go to meet Geo halfway.

"I'm sorry," Will said, his voice taut.

"Do you even know what you're apologizing for?"

Will eyed him intently. "For making you feel like you're not enough, when you're everything to me." He held Geo's gaze a moment longer, then turned and walked toward his car.

Geo drew in his breath. He felt like he'd been punched in the gut. He stood as if in a trance, watching the man he loved drive away. Will was halfway down the street when the urge to go after him hit.

But Geo couldn't do that. His self-respect was at stake. Besides, he couldn't leave Mrs. O'Leary alone.

He went into the sun room to check on her. She was sitting up and reading a book. "Sorry," he said. "Didn't realize you were awake. Can I get you something?"

"I'm fine. Was that your young man?"

Geo's face heated. "I'm sorry if we disturbed you."

"That's all right, Becca told me he was coming. She said you've been in love with him a long time."

Geo didn't know how to respond to that. What did Becca know? Had she figured out that Will Darcy was the Will from college? She couldn't have. He'd been careful not to give that away.

Mrs. O'Leary continued, "Some people say that if two people are meant to be together, it will all work out. I say that's poppycock. If two people want to be together, they have to work for it. If you love someone, and you let him get away, you'll regret it. Maybe not today, and maybe not tomorrow..."

"But soon," Geo said, looking away and sliding his hands into his pockets, "and for the rest of my life." He looked up at her and smiled. "Are you a Bogart fan?"

"Not particularly. That's a good movie, though."

They played Scrabble until Becca returned. Becca helped her mother to her room. Then, she made coffee and offered Geo some home-baked chocolate chip cookies.

They sat at the table in the kitchen nook. She said, "I got a text from Will. You two talked?"

"For a few minutes. Weren't you two supposed to meet? Why did you let him come here while you were out?"

She looked at him as if he were a twenty-five watt bulb in a sixty watt lamp. "You showed up here heartsick for the man. Two days later, I got a frantic call from him asking if I knew where you had gone. I played Cupid. So sue me."

"It's too soon. I'm not sure I'm ready—"

"You've been pining for him for ten years. You're not getting any younger. It's rare to get a second chance at love like this. Don't blow it."

He eyed her in confusion. "How did you know he was the Will from college?"

"Mandie told me. She and I have been working to save this merger. I've never seen Oscar so pissed."

"That's my fault. I should have told him from the beginning about my history with Will."

"Yes, you should have. I understand why you didn't. And there was nothing in the changes you made to the contract that I wouldn't have approved. Still, it was a conflict of interest."

"I know. I wasn't thinking clearly. That's no excuse—"

"You don't have to explain. I'm not your boss anymore. If I were, I'd have to fire you, but..."

He chuckled. "Thanks for the vote of confidence."

"Geo, I'm your biggest fan. I want you to find someone who makes you happy. It's been clear to me since you first mentioned Will that you never got over him. Don't let your pride get in the way of your future."

"It's not pride—"

"Are you sure about that? I realize he said some shitty things to you. Sometimes when couples fight, they say shitty things. Is it part of a larger pattern of behavior?"

Geo thought about that a moment. "The opposite, really. He usually treats me with respect. But this time... What bothered me most was that he called me impulsive and irresponsible, and that used to be true of me. But it's not anymore. I've grown up. It's like he's not even giving me a chance."

"Normally, I'd agree. You're not irresponsible. But in this case? Ever since you saw Will again, your behavior has not exactly been exemplary. Neither has Will's. The two of you together have done a fine job of jeopardizing this merger. And kissing in the conference room like that, with the door unlocked? It's like you *wanted* to get caught."

Geo crossed his arms, his jaw tight. He wished he could deny her assessment. But the more he thought about it...

"Huh," he said. "Maybe on some level, I did want to get caught. I was tired of the secrecy. And I hate Oscar's stupid rules."

"I know," Becca said. "That's my fault. I should have pressed him harder on it."

Geo scrubbed his face with his hands. "I don't know what to do."

"You'd better decide soon, because Will's coming over in half an hour."

"What?"

"He and I have business to discuss."

"Shit. I need to get out of here. I'm not ready to see him again."

"Don't forget about dinner. You promised Mom you'd make your famous seafood enchiladas. We bought all the ingredients."

"I'll be here." He gave her a smile before he grabbed his phone and walked out the door.

Chapter 15

As he stood in the middle of Becca's mom's family room, Will's stomach did a little flip. He glanced at his watch again and told himself to stop. Everything was under control. Candlelight, check. Catered dinner, check. String quartet, check.

It was a bit of a squeeze, fitting the instruments into the sun room. The musicians were tuning them now. Will had always liked the cacophony of it. A promise of things to come.

He was taking a risk. Geo might not like being surprised in this way. But Will had to do *something*. Fortunately, Becca had jumped at the suggestion. She and her mother were happy to go out for the evening so Will and Geo could be alone.

Will didn't mind groveling. He had lost his temper and disrespected the man he loved. Reminders of past mistakes were not part of the relationship Will wanted with him.

The doorbell rang. That was the musicians' cue. They began playing *Eine Kleine Nachtmusik*. Geo would laugh at the extravagance. Will was okay with that.

Heart pounding, he approached the entryway. The lamps inside the house were dim to show the candlelight to best effect. The overhead on the front landing shone bright, though, as he opened the door.

Geo was dressed in khaki shorts and a golf shirt that matched the Caribbean blue of his eyes. Will's heart turned to liquid. He wanted to run his fingers through that curly, golden-brown hair. To press his palm to the other man's nape and drag him in for a kiss.

But he'd lost that right. If space was what Geo needed right now, Will would give him that. Even if desire quivered inside him.

Geo arched his brows, and his lips curved into a sardonic grin. "You're joining us for dinner?"

Will took a breath to regain his composure. "It's just you and me." He threaded his fingers through the hair on the back of his head. "If you want to stay, that is."

Geo cautiously stepped inside. "Romantic."

"That was the plan." Will quirked a hopeful smile.

Geo ambled toward the sound of the music. When he caught sight of the quartet, he laughed. His eyes turned to Will. "You have way too much money."

"Probably."

Geo walked over to the dining table, where covered platters were keeping the food warm. He picked up one of the lids to reveal the meal.

Will elaborated, "Steak, mushrooms, garlic mashed potatoes, haricots verts, and sourdough bread. For dessert, chocolate cheesecake with strawberries."

Geo looked up at him. "All my favorites."

"Would you expect anything less of me?" Will teased, affecting a haughty tone.

"Of course not."

Will took a step toward him. "I know I can't buy your love. That's not what this is. I want you to relax, to enjoy yourself, without any pressure or expectations. I made a mistake, and I want a chance to make amends. Just a chance."

Geo thrust his hands into his pockets. His expression was blank, non-committal.

Like Will, Geo had grown up amid great wealth. A display like this would not impress him. Will could do this every evening for the rest of his life, and would not feel the expense.

"I'm willing to put in the time to regain your trust," Will said. "Will you let me start tonight?"

Geo stepped forward and took his hand without meeting Will's eyes. The gesture was almost shy. "Okay," Geo said softly.

Though tempted to kiss him, Will was determined to let Geo lead. He had to prove he could let go of his own rigid ideas of how things "ought" to be, and instead adapt to what Geo needed.

"Shall we eat?" Will asked.

Geo didn't answer. He massaged the back of Will's hand with his thumb, then raised it to his lips and kissed the knuckles.

"When I saw you here today," Will said, "you cannot imagine my relief." The roughness of his voice surprised him. "I didn't know where you were. I didn't know how to find you. I thought I might never see you again."

"I just needed space."

"When no one could get hold of you, Mandie and I went to your house." Will's voice cracked. "Your neighbor let the police in to make sure you weren't dead."

"I'm sorry." He sounded genuinely surprised. "I didn't mean to worry you."

It hurt Will's heart to see him feeling so alone. Will didn't know how to get through to him. "Don't you realize how much your coworkers care about you?"

"They're not my coworkers anymore."

Will took a moment to absorb that. Obviously Geo carried some bitterness about what had happened. That was understandable. But one incident didn't negate his entire career there. "They still care."

"I was embarrassed. And I didn't know what to do about *us*—I still don't. So I stopped checking my texts."

"I'm sorry." Will took both his hands. "I know it will take work to repair this relationship. Can we do that together?"

Geo's jaw worked. "I don't know if I'm ready." His eyes strayed to the table. "But I suppose it wouldn't hurt to have dinner together. And I'm kind of starving."

Will smiled, the weight in his chest lifting.

They took the covers off the platters. Geo said, "Hmm. This could be warmer."

Will stared down at his own dish. The mushrooms looked limp, and the potatoes a little crusty. Filet mignon might not have been the best choice under the circumstances.

"How well done is this steak?" Geo asked.

Will furrowed his brow in confusion. "Medium rare."

"Perfect. I can make a stir fry." Geo took his plate into the kitchen. Warily, Will followed with his own.

Geo located a heavy stainless steel skillet and turned on the gas stove. While he sliced up the beef, Will said, "I'm sorry about this."

"Why?" Geo asked, drizzling some cooking oil into the pan. He added the steak, mushrooms, and green beans. "Filet mignon is awesome this way. I'll only cook it enough to heat it through. Think you can manage to microwave the mashed potatoes?"

Will found a bowl and spooned the potatoes inside. "Your mother *did* teach me how to use a microwave."

Geo froze in the act of stirring up the entrée with a wooden spoon. A moment later, he turned off the flame.

Will set the microwave to heat for one minute, then turned and caught sight of Geo's face. His eyes were misty.

"Geo?" Will prodded.

"I forgot how close you and my mom were. I haven't had much reason to think about it over the years. You were like a son to her."

"She was like a mother to me."

Their gazes locked. A quiet understanding flowed between them, memories of a past no one could take from them. Geo's somber expression eased into a smile.

They refilled their plates and went back to the dining table. As they sat, Geo shook his head. "I can't believe you hired live music."

"I tried to get a jazz band, but couldn't find one available on such short notice."

Geo chuckled. "Classical is fine. Thank you for doing this for me."

"You're the love of my life. I would do anything for you."

Geo met his gaze. "Will…"

"That's okay. You don't have to say anything."

"You know I'm in love with you, right? I want a future with you. But right now, the past is in the way. I'm not sure how to change that."

"It'll take time," Will said. "But we can get through it."

"That's easy to say…"

"I spoke in anger. I was upset and resentful. The person I was most upset with was myself. But instead of owning that, I made a scapegoat of you. It was wrong. I would give anything to undo it. Please don't let one mistake erase everything between us."

They sat in silence a long time. Finally, Will said, "I get that this isn't just about Monday. Ten years ago, I walked out on you, and you're still carrying the scars. I won't make the same mistake again. I will follow you to the ends of the earth."

"What happened ten years ago was my fault."

"It wasn't entirely your fault. You didn't feel safe with me. You didn't trust me to have your back. That's on me."

Geo's eyes glistened, but he blinked away the tears. "With so much pain between us, how can we possibly put the past behind us?"

"We can't. I don't think we should even try. We accept our mistakes, we learn from them, and we grow. Our mistakes made us who we are now. They brought us to this place and gave us this second chance. I'm not perfect. I can still be rigid—"

"And I can still be irresponsible."

"No, Geo."

"Yes. But I've got better judgment now. I evaluate risks better. On Monday, I was thinking about the risk to myself, not to you."

"That wasn't your job. That was mine. I was the irresponsible one."

Geo gave him a wide grin. "Because I'm so irresistible?"

"You make me want to take risks. To break the rules. To live on my own terms, and to hell with everyone else. And that scares me."

The muscles in Geo's face softened. "Maybe we can find a way to meet in the middle. Someplace where you still feel safe, but you don't close yourself off to fun."

"I'd like that."

Geo sipped his sparkling water. "How are things with Oscar?"

Will let out a little chuckle. "He's no longer threatening to nullify the sale. Becca has convinced him of the futility of that. For one thing, he invested a tidy sum in his brother's winery. He wouldn't want to give that back. For another, it helped when I told him you and I had a history together—"

"You told him that?"

"At Mandie's urging, yes. The fact it wasn't a fling, as he assumed, made him more sympathetic. I told him you're the one who got away."

Geo quirked a smile. "Am I?"

"Of course you are. Oscar remembered when he introduced us, how shell-shocked I looked—" Will broke off. "Sorry. Poor choice of words. Nothing I've experienced can compare to what you and your comrades endured during your service."

"It's an expression. Most people don't think anything of it."

Will rotated his glass. "Now I'm worried I'll say something insipid, like 'Was war truly so dreadful?'"

Geo nodded thoughtfully. "It was as bad as you imagine, probably worse. But it taught me to believe in myself and my skills, and to work as part of a team. I'm a better man for the experience."

"I haven't told you how much I admire the man you've become. I should have before now. I would love for you to come work for Pemberley, but I won't pressure you if that's not what you want. "

"I need to make my own way."

"I respect that." Will hesitated before continuing, "Have you thought about moving back to Pennsylvania?" He held his breath, waiting for the answer.

Geo shrugged. "I don't have deep roots in Texas. It's been good spending time with my aunts and cousins. But Dallas isn't really home."

Will swallowed. His heart beat rapidly as he gazed deeply at the man across the table from him. This was no time to hold back. If he didn't win this man now, tonight, he might not get another chance.

"I want you with me, Geo. I realize it's only been ten days, but I've been waiting for this for ten years. I don't care about the past. We both made mistakes, but we've grown up since then. I want to move forward without recriminations. I can't promise I won't screw up again. But if I do, I'll own it. Please forgive me. You're everything to me."

Geo nodded thoughtfully. "You're asking me to move halfway across the country for you."

"I'll cover the expenses if you want. I'll arrange everything. Or if you prefer to handle it yourself, I'll stay out of it."

Geo eyed him for a long moment. "I can take care of it."

Will set his jaw, fighting the urge to argue. "As you wish." But the next moment, he realized what had just happened. "You're moving to Philadelphia?"

"I may as well," Geo said sardonically.

"If you need a place while you're looking for your own, my guest house is empty. Or you could move there permanently. Or you could move in with me." He clenched his teeth. "Or I could leave everything up to you."

Geo chuckled. "It's killing you, isn't it."

"I have the means to make your life easier. But if you don't want my help—"

"It isn't about you, Will. It's about my self-respect."

"You're a self-made man. You're not indebted to anyone for your success. Accepting my help doesn't diminish that in any way. I understand your desire for self-reliance. But you don't have anything to prove to me."

Geo pursed his lips. "I like the idea of moving in with you. I know I shouldn't—"

"Then stay in the guest house. You'll have your own space, and we can play it by ear. No pressure."

"It's a tempting offer."

"Good." Will looked at him intently. "Please, Geo."

Geo shook his head and smiled. "I can't believe I'm doing this."

Heart full to aching, Will rose and held out his hand. Geo took it and stood beside him. They gazed at one another a moment.

When Geo took a step closer, Will could resist no more. He closed the space between them and pressed their lips together. Geo grabbed Will's belt loops and dragged Will hard against him.

All Will's worries of the past three days melted into a haze of tenderness and lust. He needed this man in his bed, tonight and for the rest of his life. Geo's eager caresses conveyed his own desire.

But this was not the place, and now was not the time. The chamber orchestra was still playing just out of sight. The caterers would be there any minute to collect their serving dishes. Becca and her mom would not be far behind.

"Stay in my room tonight," Will said, lavishing kisses along Geo's neck. "Or I could come to you."

Geo chuckled. "Thanks for the offer, but I *suppose* I can stay at the Ritz with you. You're worth the sacrifice."

Will held him close, grateful beyond words to have this man in his arms again.

Chapter 16

Geo quickly packed up his things and checked out of his hotel room. Then, he followed Will's car and joined him in his luxury suite. Geo had a hundred things on his mind, but at the top of his priority list was getting Will naked.

The suite wasn't as large as the one in Dallas had been, but it was just as lavish. Light wood, blue and tan upholstery, glass-topped dining table. Geo's eyes searched for the bedroom.

Will danced him there, shedding clothes as they went. Before they reached the bed, Will backed him against the wall. Completely bare now, Will's hand found Geo's cock. Geo bucked and shivered at the contact. His palms roamed down until he cupped Will's ass and dragged their bodies hard together.

"I've missed this," Geo said on a moan. It had only been a few days, but the sadness of life without Will had left him feeling bleak. Now his world was awash with color, like a Kandinsky painting.

"Me, too," Will answered. Their mouths met in teasing kisses. The glide of tongue on tongue sent tingles over Geo's skin. He breathed in Will's familiar scent—wool and sandalwood and man. He wanted to live enveloped in it forever.

Geo fisted their cocks in one hand as Will nipped at the ball of his shoulder. The scrape of teeth against flesh awakened Geo's nerve endings.

"You're going to leave a mark," Geo warned him.

"That's the point." Will's mouth captured his in a possessive kiss.

Urgency built as Geo's balls pulled tight against his body. He needed this release, needed to fall apart in Will's arms, to surrender to him completely. He sped up the rhythm.

"That's it," Will said in a gruff voice. He bit Geo's earlobe. "Come for me."

Geo leaned back to brace himself against the wall. The quickening in his shaft warned of the impending orgasm. Wave after wave of pleasure swamped him. He convulsed and cried out, shimmering in the joy of Will's kisses.

Will finished himself off while Geo held him. Geo kissed the russet nipples as Will shot his seed between their bodies. Geo crushed against him, the sticky essence coating them.

They stood together catching their breath. Will pressed a kiss to Geo's temple, to the corner of his eye, to the apex of his cheekbone. "You're mine, Geo. Say you'll always be mine."

A hum of pleasure escaped Geo's throat. "Always."

They showered and got into bed, the cotton sheets cool and smooth. Geo nuzzled Will's neck. "I hope you've got plenty of lube," he said, "because I'm ready for round two."

Will kissed Geo's crown. "Have you ever topped?"

Geo stilled. He didn't know where this conversation was headed, and he didn't want to make any wrong assumptions. "It's something I've done. It's not something I crave."

Will didn't look at him. "I wouldn't want to deny you if it's something…" He trailed off, as if he couldn't make himself finish that sentence.

Geo caressed Will's arm, unsure what was going on, but worried it was nothing good. "I can be happy without it. I *can't* be happy if you do something sexually that you don't really want, because you're worried I'll stray if you don't."

"I don't think that."

He pressed kisses along Will's jawline. "Then what *do* you think?"

"That I'm too controlling. That I should let you lead sometimes."

Geo rested on his elbow and gave him a smirk. "There are other ways for me to take the lead." He opened the bedside drawer and found the lube and condoms. He tossed them onto the king-sized bed for easy access.

Then, he kissed his way down Will's body. Taking his time, he trailed his tongue along the ridge of a collarbone, the curve of a pectoral muscle, the valley between abdominals.

And all the while, Will threaded his fingers through Geo's hair, treating him to a hiss of pleasure, a gasp of delight, a whispered word of love. Those sounds of barely contained need made Geo even harder.

As his mouth approached Will's cock, Geo said, "I want you to lie still and let me give you pleasure. Can you do that for me?"

"I should be giving you pleasure."

"You will, I promise." Geo gave him a wicked smile. He licked his lips, and Will's prick jumped.

Geo ran his tongue over the slit, then circled the flared ridge of the head. Will let out a deep groan. Geo took his time, encompassing an inch in his wet heat, then pulling back. He repeated the slow torture until Will was writhing.

"Stop teasing," Will said tautly. "You're killing me."

"Like you always do to me." Geo accepted a little more, running his lips over the shaft before finally taking him deep into his throat. Will's back arched off the bed.

But Geo wasn't done tormenting him. Pressing a knuckle against Will's taint, he kissed his way down to Will's balls. He licked the seam and sucked them into his mouth. The ministrations up and down Will's cock continued until the man babbled inarticulately.

At last, Geo got the lube. He slicked up Will's dick, then slid two fingers inside himself.

Will groaned. "That's so hot, Geo. Sometime, I want to watch you finger yourself like that until you come."

"Another time," Geo said. "I've got plans for tonight." He kissed him, then straddled Will's lap. Positioning that long, thick cock at his entrance, he slowly slid down. The stretch fed a deep need inside him. The brush against his prostate made him shudder.

Will groaned with pleasure. Being joined with him like this was all Geo's fantasies come to life. No matter how they started, they ended with this intimate possession, this oneness of mind and body.

He slid down slowly, letting his body adjust. Fully seated, he ran his hands over Will's chest. "Perfect."

"You're so tight," Will said in a strained voice. "Can't get enough."

Geo answered by riding him in a slow rhythm. Each long stroke, up and then down, fed the pleasure, the growing heat of passion inside him. Will's face flushed, the lines taut, the eyes bright with concentration.

Will angled to stroke Geo's sweet spot, and Geo cried out with the ecstasy of it. He wanted to scold Will for his disobedience, but the friction felt too good. Their bodies worked in harmony, responding to each other, giving and receiving pleasure.

A gentle palm ran down Geo's torso and found his cock. Will took him in his large fist, rubbing a thumb over the head. The urgency built, and Geo spilled over that hand, coating Will with the thick, creamy essence.

With loud, throaty cries, Geo came and came. Will quickly followed, his face twisted in the throes of bliss. Geo kept riding, squeezing out every drop from his lover.

Finally, he collapsed on Will's chest. Will's arms wrapped around him as their heartbeats slowed. "I love you," Will said. "I've always loved you. I should never have let you go."

Joy expanded Geo's chest. "No more regrets," Geo said. "The winding path we took led us here, and I've never been happier than I am right now." He kissed Will's lips tenderly. Looking into those deep, dark eyes, he could see eternity.

Chapter 17

Will entered his penthouse in Philadelphia after work the following week. Geo was standing at the picture window looking out over the city, lights shimmering through the darkness.

He turned at the sound of Will's footsteps. Will was reminded of that moment in Dallas two weeks earlier when their eyes had met for the first time in ten years. When everything that had gone wrong in his life made the first steps toward mending.

Had it really only been two weeks?

Convincing Geo to move in with him had been a challenge at first. Geo had agreed to the guest house at the property outside the city. But during the week, Will stayed at the penthouse near his office to save on commuting time.

Geo had hesitated, joking that he didn't want to be a kept man. But Will had tortured him with kisses until he relented.

"Gorgeous view you've got here," Geo said.

"It certainly is." Will looked into Geo's breathtaking blue-green eyes.

A faint blush rose on Geo's cheeks as he seemed to comprehend the double entendre. "I admit, I miss the house with the pool. But I like that you're just steps away, so I don't have to wait hours for you to get home." He removed Will's tie, and pressed kisses to his neck.

"I hope you didn't wait here all day. I told you, my driver can take you anywhere you want to go."

"I don't like the idea of being dependent."

"You're not. There's no point in you spending your savings on an Uber when I've got a car and driver available. Besides, I'm the one who got you fired, remember? It's the least I can do."

Geo stiffened at that.

Will furrowed his brow. "Something wrong?"

"I talked to Becca today. She mentioned that...there's an opening at Pemberley for the director of corporate giving. And I remembered how your mom had run the Pemberley foundation. She was able to do that from home, and still be around for you and Ana."

Will's brows quirked up. "Are you interested?"

"I kind of am?" Geo admitted. "It's isolated from the rest of the business, its own little niche. I wouldn't worry as much about people treating me differently because we're together. And if we have kids someday..."

Will beamed. "You want to be a stay-at-home dad?"

"We both lost our parents so young. I'm grateful every day that I saw as much of my parents as I did growing up. By the time I became an adult, they were gone."

"I know." Will kissed his cheek. "I love the idea. I won't put any undue pressure on the hiring manager if you don't want me to."

"I meet the qualifications. I'd have a lot to learn, but I can do this job."

The excitement in Geo's voice made Will wonder. "Do you *want* me to talk to the hiring manager?"

"Would it be terrible if I said yes?"

Will beamed inwardly. It would be the furthest thing from terrible. He respected Geo's desire for independence. At the same time, they were a couple now, and couples took care of each other.

"You're not some boy toy I picked up at a bar. My father wanted you to work at Pemberley. My mother would be thrilled that you're following in her footsteps." Emotion gathered in his throat.

"Then let's do it."

Will smiled at that. "You're okay with accepting my help?"

Geo nodded tentatively. "We're a team now."

Will drew him in for a deep kiss. This man was everything he wanted for the rest of his life.

Geo rested his head on Will's shoulder. "I can't believe we found our way back to each other. After all the mistakes I made—"

Will pressed a finger to his lips. "No more of that. Think of the past only as it gives you pleasure."

Geo lifted his brows. "I remember so many ways of giving you pleasure. Things we haven't tried again yet. I could refresh your memory tonight."

"I wouldn't complain."

Geo took his hand and led him toward the bedroom, and all thoughts of business fled Will's mind.

Chapter 18—Epilogue

The wide receiver caught the pass in the end zone as the final buzzer sounded. The referee signaled that the touchdown was good. Chaos broke out on the field.

Geo high-fived Will in the comfort of their private suite. It had been a long time since Geo had seen a football game that exciting, and he'd never done so in such comfort. Caviar, filet mignon, and tuxedoed waiters to serve it.

Will probably could have ordered the best scotch money could buy. But Will never drank around Geo. Even though Geo had told him more than once he didn't mind. It was just one of many ways that Will put Geo first.

After nine months together, they had settled into a routine. Weekdays in the city working hard, weekends in the suburbs playing just as hard. When Will wasn't traveling, at least. But he never traveled on weekends unless he brought Geo along. He'd made that commitment, and he'd kept it.

Nine months. The time had flown by, yet it was long enough to make a baby. Which reminded Geo...

"There's something I've been meaning to talk to you about," he said to Will. "You know I've been talking to adoption attorneys, and something's come up that we need to discuss. A lot of people in our situation request healthy white babies, but that's not important to me."

Will took his hand. "To be honest, I never pictured us with white children. That's not where the greatest need is. I can understand people wanting their adopted children to look like them, but I don't care about that. It's not as if anyone will assume that you and I managed to make a baby together."

Geo smiled, happiness filling his chest. He loved that he and Will were on the same page on this. "What about special needs kids? For instance, a baby born addicted to drugs. They'll need extra love and care, but with the right therapy, they can often overcome any developmental delays."

Will turned pensive. Geo knew better than to make assumptions when it came to Will's silence. He was thinking it over, and Geo just had to be patient.

"I agree that we should be open about special needs children. We have the resources to take on extra challenges. I want to make sure we understand what we're getting into."

"Of course. I won't pressure you into something you're not comfortable with."

Will leaned in and kissed him. "You never do."

They waited an hour for the traffic leaving the stadium to clear out. Then, they crossed the Schuylkill River and headed to the house in Gladwyne.

When they got home, the place was quiet. The staff had Sundays off. "After that meal at the game," Will said, "I figured you wouldn't want a big birthday dinner. But how about," he said, taking a white box out of the refrigerator and setting it in the middle of the table in the breakfast nook, "a birthday cheesecake?"

Opening the box, Geo smiled at the sight. Chocolate cheesecake, his favorite. Fortunately, it didn't have thirty-three candles on it. They probably would have melted the cake before he could blow them all out.

Instead, it had three candles in a neat row. That seemed appropriate. And it looked like something Will would do.

Geo kissed his cheek. "I love it. Thank you."

Will lit the candles and kissed Geo. "Happy birthday, my love."

Geo blew out the tiny flames. He made a wish that he and Will would always be as happy and in love as they were on that day. But even as he wished it, he knew it would come true. Geo had faced terrible loss and hardship in his life, and come out the other side. Nothing could tear him and Will apart.

Will got a bowl of fresh strawberries out of the refrigerator, and they sat down to their dessert. It was ridiculously rich and decadent. Not overly sweet, but with the dark chocolate the perfect counterpoint to the rich cream and tart berries.

The alarm on Will's phone buzzed. He took it out of his pocket and tapped the screen to silence it. "I have one more surprise." He rose and stretched out his hand.

Geo took it, and Will led him out onto the deck. The river beyond the lawn sparkled in the moonlight. "What are we doing?" Geo asked.

"We're waiting."

"Not my strong suit, but okay."

Will chuckled. "It will be worthwhile, I promise."

Fortunately, they didn't have to wait long. When the first rocket shot into the sky and burst into a cascade of white light, Geo said, "No way."

Then, his heart clenched as Will got down on one knee.

"No way!" Geo cried, his hand trembling as he covered his mouth. It was stupid to have such a powerful reaction. He and Will were talking about adopting children together. But with fireworks going off and Will holding a ring box, Geo felt giddy. Like he might faint from so much emotion.

The sky was ablaze in light, but Geo couldn't take his eyes off Will. The man spoke in a clear, strong voice, but Geo knew by now that Will's public speaking training meant he could fake calm even when he was a ball of nerves.

Will had to pause every now and then as the fireworks boomed, drowning out his voice. The two of them were soon laughing at the absurdity of it. Finally, Will seemed to decide to cut to the chase. "Geo, you're my life. I will love you till I die. Will you marry me?"

Geo sank to his knees and kissed him, long and hard and deep. "Yes. I will marry you and spend my life making you happy."

Will slipped the ring on his finger. Geo couldn't really see it in the darkness, but he was sure he would love it. Will knew what he liked.

They kissed again before rising to their feet. Then, they stood wrapped in each other's arms, watching the show. Red and blue and green light sparkled on the water.

It was the most perfect happiness Geo had ever known. Life wouldn't be easy for them—it wasn't easy for anyone, no matter how privileged. It hadn't stopped Will and Ana from losing their parents too young. It hadn't prevented the heartache of separation Will and Geo had endured.

But now that was behind them. They never spoke of the mistakes of the past, not even when they argued. They were forging a new life together, one of great promise and absolute commitment. Geo trusted Will to be a generous husband, as he was generous in all things. The two of them had the means and the desire to make the world a better place for themselves and their children. Geo had no doubt they would succeed.

Thank you for reading *Darcy Does Dallas*! Please consider leaving a review to let others know what you thought. Want more from Andrea Dalling? Download complimentary books when you sign up for updates.

Excerpt from *The Marriage Proposal*, Book 1 in the *Poor Little Billionaires* series.
Can a fake marriage turn to true love?
CEO Noah runs a tight ship when it comes to business, but he made the ultimate workplace mistake: he dated his assistant. When the guy quit his job in a snit, he left some important paperwork unresolved—namely, Noah's visa extension. Now Noah's got two weeks to get things in order, or he'll have to leave the country.

Enter IT expert Dylan. Noah's had a secret crush on him for months. Bone-meltingly handsome and wickedly smart, Dylan's the only guy in the company who doesn't kiss up to the boss. Marrying him will solve two problems at once: Noah will be able to stay in the country, and he'll get to play house with the one guy he can't get out of his system.

Dylan's life is complicated enough without a marriage of convenience to the boss. That can't possibly end well, right? But the guy sure knows how to fill out a suit, and Dylan's had more than one fantasy about what's underneath it. Plus, Noah is offering to throw a stack of money Dylan's way. With his mom on the brink of losing her house due to medical bills, it's an offer Dylan can't refuse.

When Dylan moves into the blond-haired, blue-eyed CEO's mansion, it's supposed to be a temporary situation. But when Dylan sees the cracks in Noah's confident façade, he can't stop his heart from getting involved. Will their differences tear them apart, or can these two opposites find their way to lasting love?

This steamy gay romance has a happy ending and no cliffhanger.

Noah Harrison pressed the Esc key for the five thousandth time and swore loudly, as if the pitch and tone of his voice would make his computer behave. As CEO of the company he'd inherited from his father, Noah was accustomed to being obeyed. It pissed him off that this accumulation of circuit boards and industrial plastics wouldn't bend to his will like everyone else did.

Get a grip, he told himself, massaging the bridge of his nose. But he didn't have time to get a grip. He had a meeting in half an hour, and he needed to review the financials first.

A knock came on his door, and he looked up. His stomach bottomed out, and his mouth fell open. The most handsome man he'd ever seen was standing there, tall and slim and tanned, with dark hair and eyes. His expression was tight with apprehension, but somehow he seemed to wear a mocking smile.

"Hey, I'm Dylan McCann from IT," the god-like creature said, his voice a sexy baritone. "I understand you're having trouble?"

Noah was definitely having trouble. With his dick. It was at half-mast, which was not supposed to happen when an employee walked into his office. HR had given him shit the last time...

He set his jaw. He didn't like thinking about that.

Besides, the guy was waiting for an answer, and Noah was staring like a horny teenager. He narrowed his eyes and checked out the goods. The dude might be hot, but he looked like he was barely out of college. Noah wasn't about to trust him with his PC. "Where's Riya?"

"Out sick." Hot IT guy closed the door. "What can I do for you?"

"Call Riya and get her ass in here."

The man gave him a level look. "Unless you want her to spread her stomach flu to everyone else in the company, including you, you're stuck with me."

Noah scowled at him.

"It's okay, I'm *good*." Hot IT guy flashed a smile. "I found an issue that saved the last company I worked for two million dollars the first month I was working there."

Noah raised his brows skeptically. "Then why aren't you still working there?"

"I knew what I was worth, and they didn't want to pay it." The man's casual but confident tone fanned the fire in Noah's cock. "I had my pick of three job offers when I took this one."

Noah eyed him a moment longer, not convinced, but his options were limited. The meeting was in twenty-five minutes. "Fine."

"So let's try this again. What can I do for you?"

The guy's cocky smile made Noah want to back him against a wall and devour every inch of him. He was insubordinate as fuck, but Noah's dick seemed to like him that way. For the sake of appearances, Noah glared. "You realize I'm the CEO."

"Does that stand for cranky executive officer?"

If the man weren't so attractive, Noah might have fired him on the spot. But since all the blood in Noah's brain had traveled south, just from being close to that masculine perfection, he let it slide. "My computer is hosed."

IT guy nodded slowly. "Did you do something to it?"

"No," Noah said defensively. "Ever since I went into Regedit—"

"You fucked with the registry?" hot IT guy asked in a mock-scolding tone that made Noah's cock jump. "Are you an IT expert?"

Of course he was a computer expert. "I've got a degree in electrical engineering."

IT guy nodded slowly. "Then you understand that we have the computers set up in a particular way, so they'll work with all our systems."

The back of Noah's neck prickled with exasperation. "The stupid machine kept going to sleep every two minutes, so I fixed it."

"Sounds like you fixed it, all right. Move your ass so I can sit down."

Noah narrowed his eyes and said irritably, "I could fire you for speaking to me that way."

Hot IT guy shrugged. "Then I'll take one of those other two jobs I was offered. I only accepted the one here because the CEO is hot." The guy flashed a cheeky grin that made Noah warm all over. "If you want me to help you, then move that cute ass."

Fully hard now, Noah tried and failed to be offended. "That's sexual harassment."

"You're the CEO. If you don't like it, you can fire me."

Noah swallowed the knot in his throat, then moved his chair aside.

"Yeah, I thought so." Hot IT guy pulled up the guest chair.

Noah watched as the Roman god of technology clicked away at the keyboard. The guy's dark coloring and olive skin tone suggested he was Italian. Although, his last name hadn't sounded Italian, even though Noah couldn't remember what it was. Maybe the man had inherited his looks from his mother.

Noah watched as the man worked, trying not to be obvious. The dude didn't become any less attractive on closer inspection. Beneath a brow furrowed in concentration, his chocolate-brown eyes shone with intelligence.

Sitting so close, Noah caught the scent of sweet pine from IT guy's shampoo. It was weirdly intimate, but Noah had no desire to move away, nor did the other man seem uncomfortable. Apparently he was also gay, and thought Noah was hot, so—

"That should do it." IT guy turned the machine back over to Noah. "Check it now."

Noah did. The spreadsheet opened without a problem, and everything seemed back to normal. "Thanks," he said sheepishly.

"Any time." Hot IT guy rose, then winked on his way out.

Noah watched him go, hardly able to breathe. *Damn, that was brazen.* And for some reason, Noah had allowed it. He liked when a guy that hot spoke to him in a way he wouldn't tolerate from anyone else.

He didn't want to examine that fact too closely.

Not that it mattered. The company had fraternization rules. He couldn't sleep with the IT guy.

Could he?

No, that was crazy. He didn't even want to think about the bad press that could come from another reckless affair with an employee. So far, the fact that he was gay hadn't produced any noticeable negative effect after he took over the business. But even though Seattle was a progressive town, a sex scandal would always look worse if a gay man was involved.

Noah turned his attention back to his job and tried to put the hot guy out of his mind. But as he scanned the financials, his mind wandered. *IT guy topping him. IT guy on his knees.* If nothing else, Noah's spank bank had just received a new deposit.

But a little part of him wondered how he could turn fantasy into reality.

Dylan marched down the hallway to his office, the encounter with Noah replaying in his mind. What the hell had he just done? Flirting with the CEO? Had he lost his mind?

Despite what he'd told Noah, he needed this job. With his dad passing away suddenly a few months earlier, and his mom saddled with medical bills, he really couldn't afford to get fired right now. Those other two jobs he'd been offered would surely have been filled by now, and who knew how long it would take to find another position.

Something about Noah had attracted Dylan and brought out his dominant side. It wasn't just because the CEO's blond hair and blue eyes conjured images of sunshine and clear water. Or that his dress shirt clung to thick biceps, bringing Dylan's cock to life.

No, Dylan had seen the desire and distraction in Noah's eyes, and he couldn't help but play into it. Noah had actually *blushed,* his pale skin pinking, making him look even sexier. The big-shot billionaire CEO had been hot for him, and Dylan's primal instincts had taken over.

But that couldn't happen again. He had to show Noah that he was a hard-working, respectful employee, not a cocky sleaze ball trying to get inside the boss's pants for his own personal gain.

But, damn. Noah Harrison was *fine.* Now that Dylan was out of the presence of the pheromones the CEO was giving off, and he could think clearly—the fact was, Dylan had never met someone so attractive face-to-face. Noah was even better looking than his photos. And without his suit jacket, his lean, muscular frame looked positively lickable.

But Dylan couldn't think about it anymore. He'd probably never get that close to Noah again. His boss always handled Noah's IT. This had just been a fluke, a one-time thing. Noah would probably forget all about Dylan the next day.

If he didn't have him fired.

Want more of Noah and Dylan? Get your copy of *The Marriage Proposal*!

Share Your Thoughts

Thank you for reading *Darcy Does Dallas* by Andrea Dalling. If you enjoyed this book, please consider leaving a review. Your support means the world to our authors!

More from LoveLight Press

LoveLight Press is a small independent publisher specializing in LGBT Romance. Why not visit our website or join our mailing list to see our latest titles?
http://lovelightpress.com/

About the Author

Andrea Dalling lives in the sexy Southeast, where the summers are hot and the romance hotter. She loves to torture her characters but eventually rewards them with a happily-ever-after. Married to her college sweetheart, she is an ally and an advocate for LGBT rights. When she's not writing, she enjoys gardening at her Raleigh home and scuba diving in the clear blue waters of the Caribbean Sea.
Website: http://andreadalling.com/
Newsletter: http://eepurl.com/00WxP
Facebook:
https://www.facebook.com/andrea.dalling.romance
Twitter: https://twitter.com/andrea_dalling

More Books by Andrea Dalling

Romancing the Prince
When a European prince falls for the son of a U.S. senator, their secret romance could cause an international scandal.

College sophomore Lucas grew up as the privileged son of a powerful senator. That all changed when Lucas's indiscretion freshman year destroyed his father's chance at re-election. Now his father is being sent into political exile as ambassador to an insignificant Mediterranean island. Worse, his parents pull Lucas out of school, saying that living abroad will be a good experience. But he's sure their real goal is to somehow "ungay" him. With embassy guards watching his every move, he's practically in prison.

As the younger son of the King of Kalyphos, Prince Nicolo has been called The Spare since birth—and feels every bit as useless as the name suggests. With his responsible older brother being groomed for leadership, twenty-five-year-old Nico struggles to find meaningful work to counter his reputation as Europe's most wicked playboy prince. His rumored penchant for curvy fashion models hides a truth he doesn't dare reveal.

When Nico meets Lucas, the attraction between them is immediate and palpable. Nico offers to show Lucas the island's sights, and they can't resist the passion that soon burns between them. They both know discovery could lead to scandal and threaten the very existence of the monarchy of Kalyphos. Can they keep their affair secret? Or will their burgeoning love destroy both their families?

This sweet and steamy M/M royal romance has a happy ending and no cliffhanger.

Up and Coming
An unexpected love could cost him his dreams.
Emmett Cross doesn't have time to date. A college quarterback on a path to turning pro, he can't afford distractions, especially with the academic challenges he faces. When he's blindsided by a growing attraction to his friend Jake, he fights it—rumors that he's bisexual could wreck his draft prospects. But he can't stop thinking about the cute blond with the warm heart and gentle smile.

Biochem major Jake Schott has had a straight-boy crush on Emmett since freshman year. Emmett's cool logic is the perfect complement to Jake's sensitive nature. He's sure nothing can come of his longing—until a scorching kiss turns desire into hope. Although the tall, sexy athlete with the trim waist and thick biceps denies that there's a chance for them, his lustful looks and stolen touches tell a different story. Passion ignites between them, but Emmett insists on hiding the relationship.

When their secret threatens to come out, will Emmett give up Jake to protect his career? Or will he risk everything for love?

This steamy friends-to-lovers, straight-to-bi M/M romance is for a mature audience. It's a full-length novel with a happy ending and no cliffhanger.

www.ingramcontent.com/pod-product-compliance
Lightning Source LLC
Chambersburg PA
CBHW030226180626
46810CB00008B/2995